MOONGLOW

A Novel

By Francis Eugene Wood

For Sparrow
with warmest wishes
Francis Eugene Wood

Tip of The Moon Publishing Co.

Published by Tip-of-the-Moon Publishing Company
Farmville, Virginia

Printed by Farmville Printing
Photo of author by Christine Wood

Book design by the author and Jon Marken

First USA Printing

Email address: fewwords@moonstar.com
Website: www.tipofthemoon.com
Or write to: Tip-of-the-Moon Publishing Company
175 Crescent Road, Farmville, Virginia 23901

ISBN: 0-9746372-8-9

Acknowledgments

Thanks to my wife, Chris, for her tireless devotion to my work. Her ability to decipher my scribbling is amazing. Her eye for detail is sharp. And her lifelong fascination with crossword puzzles and a passion for the written word has afforded me a partner who is a walking dictionary and thesaurus rolled into one. I thank Tina Dean and Jon Marken for their editing skills and encouragement, and, most of all, for their friendship. Thanks to Dan Dwyer and the staff at Farmville Printing for their professionalism and commitment to producing the finest publications. It is a joy to work with such kind and talented people. Thanks to Jennifer and Jody Mask for allowing us to park in their driveway and to their yellow lab Duke for leading the way up to the overlook. Thanks to the people of Buena Vista, Virginia, for their kindness and hospitality when Chris and I came to visit. I thank God for allowing me the ability to tell my stories. And I thank you, the reader, for wanting more.

Author's Note

It was on March 22nd, 1987, when I first beheld the "beautiful view" that is Buena Vista, Virginia. My cousin Drew Johnson and I had been trout fishing along the Pedlar River in Amherst County when we decided to drive into Rockbridge County and try our luck on the little Irish Creek north of Coates Mountain. I noted in my journal that the fishing that day was not good. By late afternoon we had put our fly rods away and had driven along the Blue Ridge Parkway and onto Route 60. Instead of turning left and heading back to our homes in Buckingham, we went toward Buena Vista until we turned onto a road, where we parked the truck and struck out for a hike up a mountain. I do not recall how long we walked, but by the time the sun was descending into the western mountains, we were standing on a rock outcrop and looking down into the town of Buena Vista. I remember the blue haze that crept from the folds in the mountains and the river that flowed just west of the railroad tracks shimmering in the gold of sunset. It was such a peaceful scene that neither Drew nor I spoke until stars began to appear and street lights flickered below us. It was during those silent moments that I determined to someday write a story that would take place in that mountain community.

Later that night, I opened a map and found that my cousin and I had walked to the western side of Elephant Mountain. I would not forget it.

Although it has taken me over twenty years to return to that same outcrop, the peacefulness I felt on that evening long ago has remained.

I began writing and publishing my books in 1996, and now, with this publication, I fulfill the promise I made to myself in a moment of inspiration. The story is fiction. However, a reader familiar with the area will recognize certain names and places. Several of the characters are based on people I have known. The general description of the townspeople is based on the kindness shown to me and my wife during research visits to Buena Vista.

I have taken some liberties with the geography of the area. For example: the highland meadow near Sherrod Dane's home on Elephant Mountain is actually located on Cole Mountain in Amherst County. Although there is an Indian Gap Run, there is no Indian Gap trace beside it. I conjured that from a private road which leads up Elephant Mountain from behind the streets and avenues of Buena Vista.

Poetic references to Nessmuk are from the book *Forest Runes* by George W. Sears (Nessmuk), published by Forest and Stream Publishing Company in 1887. The verses quoted in the book are from "October" and "A Summer Night." The song "Moonglow" was written by Gill Hudson, Irving Mills, and Eddie DeLange and published by Ascap.

References include: "Buena Vista: The Bud Not Yet Blossomed, A Historical Commemorative Booklet Buena Vista Centennial 1892–1992," offered by Barbara Wilhelm; The Buena Vista Virginia website; *Remember When* 1943/1958; on-site visits, and interviews by this author and personal journal entries recorded in 1987; Trails Illustrated map of Lexington, Blue Ridge Mountains, George Washington and Jefferson National Forests; *North American Wildlife* (Readers Digest); *Country Doctor's Book of Folk Remedies & Healing Wisdom* by Paul Bergner and Davis S. Hufford, Ph.D. (Produced by National Geographic).

Dedication

This book is dedicated to the good people
of Buena Vista, Virginia, who allowed me
a "beautiful view" of their town.

Summer 1943

The boy ran swiftly along the rocky, winding trace beneath towering hardwood trees and past thick, green tangles of laurel. He bent low to the ground and barely felt the laurel branches as they swept over his back. Coming out of the thicket, he made time with a steady trot and long leaps over fallen tree branches. His bright eyes were alert for loose stones or a snake in his path. A gray fox waiting patiently for a chance at a ruffed grouse browsing nearby hunkered in the dark crevice of an upturned tree stump as the runner passed by. Its hope was dashed with the sudden explosion of leaves and feathers as the grouse flushed into the dense woods. The boy did not startle but kept his pace as he noticed the bird's glide down into a shadowy hollow.

Rays of dwindling sunlight reached into the forest as the boy burst into an open grassy terrace upon which the tallest trees cast their long shadows. He saw the sun cresting the long ridge ahead and noticed a thin, blue haze creeping up out of the hollows. His trot became a run, and in a minute he had crossed the highland clearing and re-entered the forest, where he followed a well-defined trail for a hundred yards before he turned off and disappeared among a maze of giant granite boulders. Minutes later he stepped into the leafy yard of a place he knew well.

Sherrod Dane stood still and silent. He could feel his heart pounding inside his chest. But he was not tired or breathless. He reached his hand out and touched the cool, smooth bark of a large beech tree. His heartbeat slowed. He walked around to the west side of the tree and traced a carving with his fingers. "I will love you, always." The aged letters had been carved by a delicate hand. Tears filled the boy's eyes as he read a promise made. He turned and found the flat stone walkway he and his mother had made. Forest debris covered the mossy stones, once placed so carefully. The boy pulled his damp T-shirt over his head and fanned the leaves away with it. Then he cleared the walkway to the stone steps that led up onto the front porch of the log cabin where his life had begun. Crows cawed in the distance, and a warm breeze lifted from the deep hollow that fell suddenly from the west end of the cabin.

Sherrod rubbed his eyes with his shirt, then pulled it back on and walked to the end of the porch. The witching hour had arrived and with it a beckoning for silence and contemplation known only by those who walk closely with nature. Sherrod licked his lips. He looked down into the hollow where golden sunlight reflected off trickling water. He gazed beyond the trees to where mountains rose and fell. He wondered at the mysteries that lurked in the blue folds and narrow passes.

Sherrod walked to the front door of the cabin. He put his hand on the doorknob, then paused and looked back into the yard. A strange feeling came over him, as if he was not alone. But he was not afraid—only puzzled. For a moment, he discerned something in the silence. Words. But not spoken words. Sherrod's hazel-blue eyes searched the shadows beyond the yard. He looked intently at the trunks of the oaks, beeches, and maple trees splashed in golden sunlight. There was a peaceful beauty in the silence.

The boy opened the door and stepped into the cabin. The last reaches of the sun dappled the interior of the place. Pictures and paintings on the rough-hewn walls seemed alive. Sherrod walked through the house slowly, noticing everything. It was just as it always had been. Warm and inviting. He touched the arm of a chair, her chair, beside the window overlooking the hollow and the western mountains. A book of poetry, *Forest Runes*, by Nessmuk lay on the side table. The bookmark was placed at one of her favorite poems by the old northern woodsman. "October." Sherrod opened the book at the marker and whispered a verse:

There comes a month in the weary year,
A month of leisure and peaceful rest,
When the ripe leaves fall and the air is clear—
October, the brown, the crisp, the blest.

Sherrod closed the book. A vibrant scarlet and blue woolen Indian blanket lay over the back of the sofa. The smell of burnt wood and ashes from the fireplace lured the boy over to the stone hearth, where a walnut mantle served as a display shelf for shared things between a mother and her young son. There were photos in handmade stick frames, arrowheads, a child's artwork, and a turkey feather ink pen. A little book of Sherrod's adventures written by his mother was propped between two smooth and rounded river stones. Everything was in its place. There was no dust, for Sherrod would not allow a single particle to settle.

He came to the cabin tucked away in the mountains once or twice a week, sometimes to clean and make repairs, sometimes to sit and think, and sometimes to grieve. But always to honor.

The sun slipped behind the ridge as Sherrod walked up the narrow staircase to the bedrooms. Small and cozy, they were functionally designed with ample roominess. A sixteen-pane window in his room allowed visibility for a good distance through an open forest. The boy only paused for a moment at his bedroom door. Then he walked down the hallway and stepped into his mother's bedroom. He immediately remembered her last words to him. She had carved them into the beech tree in the front yard.

Tears welled in Sherrod's eyes as he was filled with loss and helplessness. He turned and ran from the room, stumbled down the stairs, out the front door and into the yard where he fell upon his knees and wept beneath the sheltering branches of the beech tree. Words could not express his grief.

"Mama," he cried softly, his face against the cool bark of the smooth tree. "Oh, God," he whispered tearfully, "help me." Minutes passed as dusk settled into the forest. Silence permeated the shadows.

Exhausted, Sherrod leaned his back against the bowl of the great monarch, his hands upon its roots. He closed his eyes, and in the darkness he envisioned his mother's face. He saw the wisdom in her eyes and the smile that could brighten his day. He imagined her voice. "I will love you, always." Slowly the boy opened his eyes and saw a brilliant, full moon rising over the rooftop of the cabin. He blinked his eyes in disbelief. Then a calmness came over him. "God," the boy whispered. He closed his eyes again and prayed in silence.

On that same night two hundred miles away, a young girl strummed the last chord on her guitar, then gently leaned it against the wall next to her bedroom window. The dim light from the small lamp on her dresser brought an elegance to the old instrument that daylight did not allow.

The Silvertone guitar, a Sears and Roebuck catalog favorite, had passed through several owners before it came into the possession of Abby Rhode. It was a gift from her parents on her eighth birthday. Her mother had found it among the chairs, tables, and over-filled cardboard boxes in the front yard of a family who was moving away. The guitar had no strings when Vivian Rhode first saw it. It was also dusty and a little battered. She called it "neglected."

Abby's dad shined it up with furniture polish and had a local musician friend put on Black Diamond strings and tune it. That same musician taught Abby her first chords and how to tune the strings. That was all Abby needed. She practiced every day and played into the night, long after her parents had gone to bed. She bought a guitar chord book with money she had saved from raking yards. And in a few months, she had mastered every chord in the book. She watched local musicians play whenever she could and learned from them. She practiced until her fingers bled. Then she would wait impatiently for a couple of days for them to heal enough so that she could continue.

Abby loved music. All music. She had an ear for it and could pick out the notes easily. Her mother said it was a gift that God had given her. Vivian Rhode also loved music. She had never learned to play an instrument, but she had a lovely voice and sang in the choir at church. She also sang songs she heard on the radio. Abby had grown up hearing her mother sing around the house and sometimes her father would join in. He could barely hold a tune, but there was joy in his effort.

John Rhode was a quiet man who operated a hardware store he had inherited from his father after a heart attack took the man away at an early age. John's hours were long and arduous, but he worked with a determination to provide for his mother and his wife and child. Always out of the house before daylight, he seldom came home until long after dinner. That was when he would read stories to his daughter and tell her and her mother the events of his day. That is when he tried to make up for lost time. Sunday was always special. Some would have called it normal. But to Abby it was not normal at all. On Sunday, she awoke to the smell of coffee and bacon and the voices of her parents downstairs in the kitchen. On Sunday, they all had breakfast together. They dressed for church and picked up her grandmother and sat together on a hard, wooden pew. Vivian sat with the choir most Sundays, and Abby was always so proud of her. She could pick out her mother's voice from among the other female singers. On extra special Sundays, Vivian sang solo. Abby once saw a tear roll down her father's cheek during a particularly beautiful song by his wife. That Sunday morning he held the hands of his mother and daughter as if he could not bear to let them go.

Soon after that day, the house became quieter. There was less singing and laughter. Abby would lie in her bed and listen to her parents as they talked into the night. Soft murmurs. Nights seemed longer, darker.

John Rhode left the house later in the mornings and came home earlier. But the stories stopped. He seemed tired. His wife and mother spent more time helping him at the store.

Abby put on her nightgown and was brushing her long, black hair when she heard her mother at her bedroom door. "Abby?" the woman asked softly as she peeked around the door. "Are you about ready for bed?" The girl watched the reflection of her mother's approach in her mirror. "Just about," she answered.

Vivian took the brush from Abby's hand and continued brushing her hair.

Abby looked down and traced a flower print on her gown with her index finger. "Mama," she finally spoke. "You need to tell me about Daddy." She reached her hand back and gently took the brush from Vivian's hand. Then she turned around and looked up into her eyes. "I know something is wrong. I can feel it." The girl swallowed and tried to hold back her tears. "He's tired all the time. But, why? Tell me."

Vivian could see the worry on Abby's face. She saw the tears in her eyes. She heard the fear in her voice. She bit her lip and with trembling hands pulled Abby's face against her stomach. "Will you be strong for me, Abby?" she asked in an emotional voice.

Abby pressed her face against her mother for a moment, then wiped her eyes with her fingers. "You know I will, Mama."

Vivian knelt and grasped the hands of her daughter. She squeezed them, then held them lightly between her thumbs and fingers. "Daddy is sick, sweetheart.

He is sick with the same illness that took your grandfather from us."

Tears welled in Abby's eyes. "His heart?" she whispered.

"Yes. His heart."

Abby did not ask another question. She knew the answer already. Instead, she stood up, wrapped her arms around her mother's neck, and wept softly. "We'll pray, Mama," she said through her tears. "I'll be strong for you," she promised. "And I'll be strong for him, too."

"I know you will," her mother cried. "I've known it all along."

Minutes later, Vivian turned off the lamp on Abby's dresser and walked over to the bed and kissed the girl on the forehead. "Goodnight, sweetheart," she said as she stroked the girl's temple with the back of her fingers.

"What's Daddy's favorite song, Mama?" Abby raised up on her elbows.

Her mother thought for only a moment before she answered. "Moonglow," she smiled as she spoke. "I sang it to him under a full moon one night."

Abby looked toward the window. "Look, Mama."

Vivian reached over and pulled back the drapes. She stood in awe as moonlight filled the room.

"Was it like that?" Abby sat up in the bed and took in the scene.

But it was another voice that answered. "It was just like that, Abby," her father said as he entered the room and walked around the foot of his daughter's bed. "And your mother was just as beautiful."

"You remember?" Vivian asked as she reached out to her husband.

"How could I forget?" He smiled and pulled her to him.

For a moment Abby watched as her parents stood quietly in each other's arms. She did not speak or move for fear that the perfection of the moment would be spoiled. She could feel the love between them in those precious seconds, and somehow she knew that she would never forget this night. And when her mother began to sing, Abby put her fingers to her lips and smiled.

It must have been moonglow
Way up in the blue.
It must have been moonglow
That led me straight to you.
I still hear you singing
Dear one, hold me fast.
And I start in praying
Oh, Lord, please let this last…

The couple swayed as Vivian sang through the sadness of her heart:

We seemed to float right through the air
Heavenly songs seemed to come from everywhere
And now when there's moonglow
Way up in the blue.
I always remember that moonglow gave me you.

The last line of the song was finished in her mother's broken whisper. "I will love you, always," Abby heard her father promise his wife.

Later that night, Abby sat on the edge of her bed, and in the brilliance of the full moon picked up her guitar and played the song she would never forget. She repeated the promise made by her father and prayed that, someday, someone would love her as much as he did her mother.

The phone rang three times before Emily Tynes made it out of the kitchen and down the long hallway.

"Sherrod," she called while wiping her hands on her apron. She looked upstairs but there was no answer and only darkness in the boy's room at the head of the staircase. Emily picked up the receiver. "Hello, Doctor Tynes' residence," she said in a pleasant voice.

"Oh, Emily. This is Lucy Marsden up on Indian Gap Run." The woman's voice was husky and breathless.

Emily heard the backdoor open and stepped back to see her husband enter the house. She held up one finger. Frank Tynes looked at his wife standing beside the phone table and raised his eyebrows. Instinct told him not to remove his coat.

"Yes, Lucy." Emily watched her husband while she spoke. "Is there a problem?"

"Well, it's Woody. He's done fell backwards off his tractor and sprung his back somethin' awful. It was all I could do to git him in the house and...."

Emily motioned for her husband to come to the phone. "Lucy," she interrupted the worried woman. "Lucy, hold on, I'm going to let you speak to Dr. Tynes. He just walked in."

Emily handed the phone to her husband. "It's Lucy Marsden, Frank. She says Woodrow has fallen and hurt his back."

Frank Tynes took the phone from his wife and squeezed her hand as she turned to walk away. "Lucy?" he held the phone close to his ear. "Where is Woodrow now?"

"Doc, I've done helped him into the house, and he's layin' flat on the bed. He won't move for fear of a pain." The woman sighed. "I'm about worried to death, Doc. Kin you come take a look at him?"

The doctor pulled his coat back and lifted the gold watch from his vest pocket, just as the grandfather clock in the entrance foyer chimed the half hour. It was 6:30 p.m. He looked toward the kitchen door where Emily stood with arms folded. He smiled apologetically and put up his hand in resignation.

"Don't worry, Lucy. I'll be there soon."

He could hear the woman's sigh of relief. "Oh, thank you, Doc. I'll tell Woody you're on the way."

"All right, Lucy. Sit tight." The man hung up the phone and walked slowly down the hallway to where his wife stood at the kitchen doorway. She smiled and shook her head. Emily Tynes was not angry. Just a little disappointed. She straightened the collar of her husband's coat and leaned into his embrace. "I'll hold supper," she said.

Frank closed his eyes for a moment and smelled the fragrance of her hair. He squeezed her, then kissed her softly on the lips. "I'll be home as soon as possible, Em." He peeked into the kitchen and smiled through closed lips. "What am I putting on hold tonight?"

Emily stepped back and placed her hands on her hips. "Well, Doctor Tynes, at some time this evening, we'll be dining on baked pineapple and ham, fresh butter beans from my little garden out back, mashed potatoes with red gravy and buttermilk biscuits."

"How about one for the road?" Frank watched as Emily turned and walked over to the oven. "I'll have it for you in a sec." She opened the oven door and pulled out the tray of biscuits.

Frank's mouth watered. He turned and called, "Sherrod."

Emily spoke without turning around. "He's not home yet. You'd better grab his jacket off the rack in the hallway and take it with you. He's probably up on the mountain. He said he was going to check on things up there after school today."

Frank pulled the boy's jacket off the coat rack and laid it over his arm.

Emily finished wrapping two hot ham biscuits in a clean, white linen cloth. She walked over and gently placed the biscuits in her husband's coat pocket. "There," she said. "One for you and one for him."

"I'll talk to him, Em."

Emily shook her head. "I'm only concerned when he's out after dark. I know he's got to go up there. I'm okay with that." Emily spoke softly as she touched her husband's lapel. "It's just that I worry about him." There was emotion in her voice. "He's like my own...." She stopped and lowered her eyes.

Frank sensed the breaking of his wife's heart. He knew how much the boy meant to her. But he could not imagine the extent of Emily's love, or the suffering she endured.

He placed a finger under Emily's chin and raised her face. Her brown eyes were dark and moist. A sadness he could not deny swam in the depth of her gaze. He could see and feel it. But he could never find the words to address it.

"We'll be home soon, Em," he promised.

Emily pressed her lips together and nodded. "And I'll be waiting for you." She touched her husband's cheek with her fingers, then watched as he turned and left.

When Sherrod opened his eyes, the full moon was well above the rooftop of the cabin. He felt sluggish as he rose to his feet. It was as if he had awakened from a deep sleep. But it could have been only a few minutes since he had come out of the house and lain against the tree. He leaned against the beech tree with one hand and steadied himself. He shook his head and rubbed his temples with his free hand. His legs were weak. The boy recalled running from the house and falling to his knees. He remembered his weeping and his overwhelming feeling of helplessness. Then there was the silence and the glow of the moon.

A plea. A voice, soft and elegant. Reassuring whispers from shadowed places. Sherrod Dane laid his other hand on the bark of the tree and leaned his body against it. This was an instinctive action the boy did not understand. The smooth bark was cool on his cheek. Moments passed. Silence. And then the smell of the forest and the sounds of the night came to him as he had never experienced them. With eyes closed, he was mesmerized with things normally taken for granted. The sound of a beetle's progress beneath a leafy forest rug, and the flapping of a bat's wings as it darted among tree branches over his head. The pungent scent of soil, rotting leaves, and the fragrance of wild flowers that wafted on the warm breeze from the meadow a quarter of a mile away.

He could hear the rustling of summer leaves high in the treetops and the gurgle and trickle of the stream far down in the hollow. Creatures of the night lurked near and far in the shadows, and he saw them, furred and feathered with his mind's eye.

The sound of the wind seemed like a whisper. The whisper became a voice. But Sherrod was not afraid, for he had heard it before. Perhaps it was in a dream. Somehow it brought him comfort.

Images of his past flashed in his mind. Other images were unknown to him, but he sensed they were beyond the present. There was music, and the face of a beautiful child bathed in moonlight. And then there were faceless people, sick and frightened, wandering through a forest. Some wept and reached out their hands to him.

Sherrod pushed away from the tree with all of his strength. Instantly, the sounds and images left him. His heart pounded as he looked up at the moon and wiped his face with his hands. For a minute he stood still and noticed how the moon's glow touched his skin just as it did the bark of the beech trees, the maples and the poplars. Then he remembered a soft and elegant voice. Sherrod yearned to hear it again. He turned back toward the tree and placed his hands on it, closed his eyes and waited.

When Dr. Frank Tynes turned off the hard-surfaced road and onto Indian Gap trace, he was amazed at how narrow and rocky it was up to the Marsden's place. The last time he'd made that trip he had driven his old rugged '35 Ford truck and not a fine 1942 Cruiser. The thought occurred to him that he should have driven the truck. "Well, it's too late now, Doc," he said aloud to himself. The winding dirt road was still referred to by most people as a trace because that is just what it amounted to when Woodrow Marsden walked up the mountain back in 1899 and carved out a place on the north side of Indian Gap Run for his family farm. Woodrow had tired of tannery work and had scrimped and saved for years with the goal of buying enough acreage to farm and sustain him and Lucy.

Woodrow was a stubborn and independent man. Odd and introverted, he came into the village only twice a year. And then it was on a mule-drawn wagon. He would not own a car or truck, and it was years before he broke down and bought a used tractor. The people he saw at the mill and feed-and-seed store were his only human contacts with the outside world. He could not read, but kept up with current events, especially the war, by listening to a battery-run radio. He also listened to the Grand Old Opry and could play songs by ear on the guitar. The word on the street was that Woodrow Marsden was a fine guitar picker. But few had ever heard him play.

Doc had heard Woodrow play his guitar on a few occasions over the years. The tunes were mostly in the place of money he did not have to pay for a home call from the doctor.

"Just play me a tune, Woodrow," Doc would request as he relaxed in a rocking chair in front of the Marsden's big mud and stone fireplace after tending to an injury or an illness. The doctor would light the sweet-smelling cherry blend tobacco in the shallow bowl of his long-stemmed English reading pipe and puff gently as Woodrow would lay into old favorites such as "The Gray Speckled Bird" and "Wayfaring Stranger."

Doc smiled as he remembered his visits to the Marsden farm over the years. He could recall the music and the canned vegetables and jars of wild honey that Lucy had insisted he take home as payment for services rendered.

Frank Tynes was a country doctor whose wealth was determined by the trust, respect, and generosity of his patients in and around the town of Buena Vista, Virginia. Moneywise he was considered wealthy. But the true richness of his life was beyond even his own understanding. For there were dark places within him, and he lived in fear of the reckoning he knew would someday come.

The instruments in his black bag clinked and rattled as Doc steered the car around a sharp bend. A two-day rain early in the week had washed long ruts across the width of the trace. He drove slowly and in low gear so he would not burn out his brakes. Suddenly there was motion on the road bank to his right. Doc pressed hard on the brakes and felt the car skid forward as a deer leaped across the road just feet from his headlights. He watched the deer disappear into the blackness of the forest. Then he let off the brakes and accelerated the car up a steep incline, around another sharp bend and onto a flat. That is where he noticed the moon for the first time that evening. It was full and brilliant. The mountains had hidden it from his view until he came to a saddle of Elephant Mountain. Doc cut the car's engine and turned off the headlights. He opened the car door and stepped out. With closed eyes he allowed the moon's glow to penetrate his eyelids. A full minute passed. A dog barked twice in the distance.

Frank opened his eyes and looked through the woods to his left. "Pete," he said in a low voice.

Another bark echoed from the same direction. "Re-Pete." He smiled as he said the name. They were Woodrow's coon dogs. Frank had known them since they were pups. He reached into the car and brought out his bag. He tucked a flashlight into his coat pocket and shut the car door. Leaves shuffled, and Frank trained his sight onto a trail across the trace that led up into the woods. He knew the path well and the clearing beyond it.

"Sherrod," he called out. He listened as the shuffling sound stopped for a moment, then continued. Frank strained his eyes and waited until the boy appeared at the mouth of the dark trail. His white T- shirt seemed ghostly under the glow of the moon. Without speaking, the boy walked directly toward the car. Frank walked around to the front of the car and waited until the boy stopped in front of him.

"It's late, Sherrod," the man said. "Em's worried."

Sherrod looked up and shook his head slightly. "I'm sorry, Doc. I meant to be home before dark."

Frank studied the boy's face in the moonglow as he spoke. "You know she worries about your being out here in these mountains alone in the dark."

"I know." Sherrod looked at the man's face as he answered. "I fell asleep."

"Asleep?"

"I guess so. I woke up in the yard and, well...."

Frank felt the boy's forehead with the back of his hand. "You feel all right?" he asked.

"Yes. I guess I do." Sherrod leaned against the car.

"Is everything all right up there?" Frank looked toward the trail from which the boy had come.

"It's fine."

Frank put his hand on Sherrod's shoulder. "Listen. I'm going to walk over to the Marsden's place for a few minutes. Woodrow fell off his tractor and hurt his back. You want to come along?"

"Sure, Doc."

Frank patted the boy's shoulder. He walked back around to the driver's side of the car and retrieved the jacket Emily had sent with him. "It sure is a nice evening for a walk in the hills." He reached into his coat pocket and brought out the ham biscuits and handed one to Sherrod. Then he turned and started down the road.

Sherrod took a bite of the warm biscuit and followed the doctor down the trace toward the rushing sound of Indian Gap Run. Minutes later, they crossed a narrow foot bridge and stepped into the front yard of the Marsden place.

The coon dogs, Pete and Re-Pete, approached them in front of the house. The dogs barked and howled until they caught scent of the man and boy. Then they pestered the two humans until they stepped up on the porch and the door opened.

"Hey, Doc." Lucy opened the door wide and stepped to the side. "Thank you for comin' up. He's a hurtin' in there." The woman pointed toward the bedroom as she patted Sherrod on the back. "How you doin', Sherrod?" she asked as she closed the door behind him.

Sherrod smiled and looked at the woman's face as he answered. "I'm fine, Miss Marsden."

Lucy nervously rubbed the backs of her hands. "My goodness, boy. You done growed!"

Sherrod smiled and scratched the side of his head.

"How old are you now?" Lucy had to step back and turn her head to look up at the boy.

"I'm thirteen."

Lucy's eyes opened wide. "Well now, I reckon you are ever bit of it. Why, I recollect when you were born, and me and Woody come up there and…."

Woodrow issued a loud moan from the bedroom, and Lucy stopped in mid-sentence. She patted Sherrod on the chest with one hand. "Sit down now and I'll fetch you some milk and cookies in a minute." She hurried into the bedroom.

Sherrod followed the woman to the bedroom door where he stopped. He leaned against the painted door frame and watched and listened.

"There now, Woodrow." Frank patted the old man on his forearm. "These pills are going to ease your pain."

"When kin I git up from here, Doc? There's work to be done."

Frank closed his bag and stood up. He looked at Lucy, then down at her husband. "Your back is worn out, Woodrow. You know, I've told you for years that the discs in your spine have been degenerating."

"I know what you've said to me." Woodrow looked at his wife helplessly. He saw the worry on her face. "But when will I be well enough to git up?" There was a plea in the old man's question as well as a tear in his eye.

Frank shook his head. "Woodrow," he started slowly and chose his words carefully. "We are going to have to take some x-rays. This fall today has aggravated what was already a bad situation. I want to see the extent of the problem."

"I cain't come off the mountain, Doc!" Woodrow spoke fearfully. "I won't make it, I know it."

Lucy sat on the edge of the bed and held her husband's hand. "Don't talk like that, Woody," she scolded. "We'll do what has to be done. And if'n the doc says it's the best thing, then...."

Woodrow squeezed his wife's hand and shook his head.

Lucy gently rubbed his fingers.

Frank placed his hand on the woman's shoulder. "Keep him on his back, Lucy, and give him the pills every four hours. I'll come back tomorrow, and we'll make some arrangements."

Lucy nodded her head but did not take her eyes away from her husband's face.

Frank bent down and helped her up.

"You rest now, Woodrow. And I'm going to give Lucy some instructions on your care while I'm away."

Woodrow nodded his head in silence.

Sherrod could sense Lucy's fear and grief as she followed the doctor out of the bedroom. For a second, she lifted her eyes and silently conveyed her hopelessness to the boy.

A minute later he listened as she wept softly in the den while the doctor comforted her.

"I'm an old spent mule, boy." Woodrow spoke just loud enough for Sherrod to hear.

The boy put his hands in his pockets and walked over to the bed. "Do you really think that, Mr. Marsden?" Sherrod wanted to know the old man's answer. Woodrow forced a smile. "Doc thinks it. Lucy don't want to, but fears it's true." He closed his eyes for a moment, then opened them and looked up at the ceiling. "I feel like there's more here for me to do. I jest have that feelin'."

He turned his head and looked into the hazel-blue eyes of the boy standing near him. "I'm 87 year old, Sherrod. But if'n all I got left is to lay here in bed and stare at the ceilin', then there ain't no use in livin'."

Sherrod walked over to the open window and looked out into the moonlit forest. A warm breeze swept over the ancient mountains. It brushed the folds in the hills and lifted out of the blue and mysterious hollows. The boy took his hands from his pockets and felt the breeze on his palms. Soft linen curtains swirled in the air around him as he closed his eyes and waited in silence.

When finally Sherrod walked back over to the bed, Woodrow's eyes were closed. The old man had fallen asleep. Sherrod leaned over and whispered something. Then he placed his hand on the man's chest and closed his eyes.

Frank was still consoling Lucy in the den in front of the fireplace when she gasped and looked past him. An incredulous look came over her face as she raised her fingers to her mouth. "Woody!" she exclaimed, staring toward the bedroom door. "How did you...? What's happened?" She rushed over to him.

Frank Tynes turned and saw the old man standing straight and proud in the doorway. Woodrow Marsden's eyes were bright and alive, and a grin stretched across his face. "Turn on the radio, Lucy." Woodrow hugged his wife and laughed out loud. "I feel like dancin' with my favorite gal."

Doc was speechless! He sat down in a rocking chair, his mouth open. The only word that came to his mind as he watched the happy old couple dance beside the radio was "miracle." And that was something he had never believed in, until now.

Spring 1958

The sun was just beginning to peek from behind dark clouds as Abby Rhode pulled her little red Corvair up to the gas pumps of Glass's Service Station off of Route 501 in Buena Vista. She turned off the engine but continued listening to the Everly Brothers sing "All I Have to do is Dream" on the radio as she searched the contents of her pocketbook for her wallet.

A soft knock on her car window drew her attention to a man standing in a bent position at her door. Daniel Glass was the name sewn onto his shirt above the breast pocket. Abby smiled and switched her key to the "off" position. The sweet harmony of the Everly Brothers was cut in mid-dream as the young woman lifted her wallet from the pocketbook and rolled down her window.

"What'll it be, little lady?" The man's voice was jovial enough. His smile seemed sincere.

"Yes, sir," Abby responded as she leaned into her car door and looked up at the attendant who was now standing straight. "Could you give me five gallons of regular?" she asked.

"Yes, ma'am. I'll be glad to." Daniel Glass walked around the back of the car.

Abby closed her eyes for a few seconds, then opened them and thumbed through the bills in her wallet. A hundred dollars. She was fine on cash. Her thin, blue checkbook was zipped in a side compartment of her purse. The money in her checking account gave her a sense of security. There was plenty of money there.

She waited as the man cleaned the front and back windows of her car. A black Bel Air pulled up on the other side of the gas pumps. A dark-haired man with cruel eyes opened his car door and stepped out laughing. He bent down and said something to a pretty blonde girl who was sitting in the middle of the seat. Abby glanced at the man and his passenger and thought the girl looked much too young to be with him.

"Hey, Mr. Glass," the man called as he turned and walked toward the station door. Abby noticed the man staring at her as he walked away, and an uneasiness came over her.

"I'll be with you in a minute," the service station attendant called from behind the raised hood of Abby's car. He wiped the ramrod of her oil cap with a stained blue cloth and returned it to its place.

The dark-haired man disappeared into the station and emerged shortly with two dripping wet soda bottles in his hands. He held them up. "I got two 7 Ups," he said as he reached in his car and handed one to the girl. "The money is next to the cash register."

"Thanks." Daniel Glass closed the hood of Abby's

car, stuck the oil rag in his back pocket, and watched as the Bel Air pulled away. He shook his head slightly, and Abby saw on his face a hint of disgust.

The driver made an effort to smile at Abby as he drove past her car. She caught his effort. It felt cold and penetrating. She did not respond.

"Oil looks good, ma'am." Mr. Glass was standing by her car window. "And I put some air in that back right tire. It was a little low."

"Oh, thanks." Abby opened her wallet. "How much do I owe you?"

"That'll be a dollar twenty, ma'am."

Abby gave the man a dollar bill and two dimes. "You know, I think I'll have a Coke," she said, opening the car door.

"I'll get it for you, little lady."

Abby got out of her car and stood up. It felt good to stretch her legs. "Thanks, sir." She walked around the front of her car and followed the man into the station. He held the door as she stepped inside.

"You been on the road for long?" he asked.

Abby watched as he opened the lid on the Coca Cola cooler. Steam rose off the cold water as Mr. Glass pulled a Coke out and dried it off with a clean rag that hung on the wall close by. He popped the top off and handed it to the woman.

"Thank you." Abby took a sip of the ice cold soda. "Well, I left Newport News this morning and only stopped twice on the way. Once, to eat at a place called Sprouse's Corner, and then again at the overlook above the town to see what I was coming into."

She smiled and took another sip of her Coke.

Daniel Glass took the dime Abby handed him and walked over to the cash register.

"You've come right many miles today, haven't you?" Daniel Glass thought that perhaps the young woman was a teacher. "I'll bet you're a teacher at Southern Seminary." The man smiled and leaned his elbows on the counter, waiting for a confession.

Abby shook her head. "Oh, no. I'm not a teacher. I graduated from National Business College in Roanoke in '55. My folks owned a hardware store in Newport News for years, and I worked there until, well…." She paused and looked outside where the sun had finally chased away the clouds.

Daniel Glass sensed the sudden sadness that had come over the young woman. He drummed his thumbs on the countertop and raised up. "You know what, miss…?" he raised his eyebrows in question.

"Rhode. My name is Abby Rhode." Abby blinked her eyes and smiled. "Please call me Abby."

The man nodded his head and showed a fatherly smile. "You've come to a good town, Abby," he said reassuringly. "It's a small town with a lot of good people. And whether you're passing through or you're gonna stay a while, you're gonna find it okay here."

Daniel Glass was not sure whether Abby was running away from something or searching for something. But he knew instinctively that she was a good person and perhaps a little lonely.

"I am going to stay for at least a while, Mr. uh…."

"Glass," Daniel finished her sentence. "I own this place."

Abby looked again at the name on the man's shirt. "Well, Mr. Glass, I'm not in the hardware business anymore. I'm going to write a book. And I want to write it here in Buena Vista." A feeling of relief came over Abby as she spoke. Finally she had said it to someone other than her mother, and it felt good.

Daniel Glass was impressed. "Well, all right, then. What is your book about?"

Abby crinkled her nose. "That's a bit of a problem at this point."

"Oh?"

"Yes, well, you see, I haven't decided that yet. But a lot of ideas have been forming in my mind for some time now. And I know, somehow, that this is where I'm going to do it."

"Why this town?" Daniel was curious.

Abby put up her hands and shook her head. "I'm not really sure," she admitted. "I only came through here once, and that was years ago when my mother and I were coming from National Business College. We didn't even stop, but there was just something about this place that drew my interest." Abby paused for a moment as if she were searching for the right words. "I just feel the need to be here."

The service station owner looked at Abby Rhode. She was a young woman who would catch the attention of any man. Shapely in her dark slacks and tan cardigan sweater, she moved with a confidence that belied her seeming indecisiveness concerning her book. And yet, there was an underlying vulnerability about her that could either draw forth a man's protective nature or his deceitfulness. Daniel Glass suspected she had known both in her life.

That she was beautiful, there was no doubt. There was a healthful glow to her fair complexion. Her nose and lips were perfect. And her eyes were blue and penetrating. Her black, shoulder-length hair was swept back as if by the wind, and her long, dark eyelashes purveyed a sensuality she might not intend. But there was something else about Abby Rhode. It was in her voice and the sparkle of her eyes when she smiled. It would stave off the inherent jealousies of other women and draw the attention and praise of even the most skeptical of critics.

Daniel Glass saw it the moment Abby smiled and spoke to him. An instant friend. An attribute not so common in an untrusting world. Abby had it. She had to be born with it. One does not acquire it in a single lifetime — not ever to know a stranger. Accepted. Strength and vulnerability. The stirrups in which friendships stand.

"Well, I'm glad you found us, Abby." Daniel meant his words. "Do you have a place to stay? There's Barnes Motel, and…."

Abby put up her hand and shook her head. "I'm going to be staying with the Tynes family. I think they live on Chestnut Avenue and Twenty-first Street."

"They do." Daniel looked surprised.

Abby saw it on his face. She explained. "A friend of mine from Lexington saw that Dr. Tynes had placed an ad in the local paper here for someone to sit with his wife and help with his practice. When I contacted him and told him my business background, he seemed excited. He said that his wife had also been his business manager for years and is now unable to handle it."

Daniel nodded his head sadly. "Yes, Emily Tynes has been going back for a while now. I saw the ad in the paper." He paused for a moment, then smiled at Abby. "Well, they are gonna love you," he said. "Tell 'em I said howdy. I don't see Doc much these days. He's semi-retired, you know. And I've been pretty healthy."

"I will." Abby raised her hand to push open the door.

Daniel rushed forward and grabbed the door handle and pushed it open as he stepped to one side. "It's been nice talking with you, Abby." He followed the woman out to her car.

"Thank you, Mr. Glass." Abby got into her car and started the engine. "Where do I go from here?"

"You just take a left out of here and go over to Twenty-first Street, go two blocks to Chestnut Avenue, and it's the big white house with the wrap-around porch on the corner. You can't miss it."

Abby put her car in gear and let off the brake. "Thanks, again. I'll be back for gas when I need it." She waved her hand and rolled up her window. Seconds later, she pulled out onto the main road.

Daniel watched Abby leave. The late afternoon sun felt good on his shoulders. He looked up at the mountains that surrounded Buena Vista. "You picked a pretty place to write your book, Abby Rhode," he said quietly.

A pickup truck turned off the road and pulled over to the gas pumps. Daniel waved at the driver and went back to work.

Doctor Frank Tynes heard the motor of Abby's Corvair as she pulled up to the curb in front of the house. He folded the newspaper he was reading and tucked his glasses in his vest pocket as he stood up.

"Who is it, Doc?" Emily looked up from her knitting and glanced toward the den window.

"That just might be our girl, Em." Doc walked over to the window and peered through the blinds. "I believe it is her." He smiled and looked back at his wife.

Emily placed the sweater she was knitting in a woven basket on the couch next to her and straightened the afghan over her legs. She corrected her posture and fiddled with her hair. "Go bring her in, Doc." Her voice was soft, but with a hint of excitement. "Does the house look all right?"

Doc chuckled. "It looks just fine, Em," he assured her. "Don't you worry."

Emily fingered the edge of the afghan nervously. "I want to stand at the door with you, Frank."

The doctor looked at his wife. Her frailness was

hidden beneath a black turtleneck and a thin, linen jacket. The fullness of her womanly features was gone. Her pale cheeks were brought to life with a touch of rouge, and her dark, brown eyes which still glittered at times were ringed in the shadow of her illness. But there was grace in her weakness and determination in her strength. Emily pulled the afghan off her legs and leaned forward as Doc helped her to her feet.

"There," he said softly. "We'll meet her at the door." Doc walked beside his wife, holding her left hand in his and supporting her weight as she leaned against him.

Abby stood on the sidewalk with her suitcase at her side as she admired the two-story Victorian house. A wide, brick walkway bordered by well-kept ivy led up to a wide porch that wrapped around the freshly painted structure. A waist-high bannister enclosed the porch which was painted a dark blue. Wooden rocking chairs, glass-top side tables, and gliders were placed at various intervals. Two porch swings hung from long chains. A dark-shingled roof covered the porch, and the woodwork that adorned the eaves and corners of the house was detailed and intricate. The pitch of the roof was steep. Brick chimneys rose at either end of the house and from its center. Large trees with sweeping branches stood like guardians at the sides and rear of the house.

Abby put down her luggage and was about to knock when the front door opened and two people smiled, said her name, and welcomed her with open arms.

Abby settled well into her new life as May began in Buena Vista. Each day seemed like a new beginning. Her nights were never long, and her days were never long enough. There was so much to do and learn. So much to see. Sometimes she felt as if she were a butterfly that had emerged into a new garden where everything was new and exciting. Her cocoon was in a place of noise and concrete, where people separated themselves from nature and locked themselves into lifestyles of mechanical existence, their senses deadened to the true world around them.

But here in the mountains the air was sweet. The fragrance of a flower could not go unnoticed, especially by a butterfly.

Abby watched the days come alive from her bedroom window on the second floor of the Tynes' home. She took her morning walks early before Jesse Lou, the cook, could even finish preparing breakfast. By the time she arrived back at the house, the aroma of coffee brewing had started the buzz of the day. Jesse Lou set the table, poured the coffee, and brought a smorgasbord of food to the table. On a typical morning there would be eggs, bacon or sausage, grits, hash browns, biscuits and white gravy, and toast with jams, jellies, and honey. Oatmeal was an option, but boxed cereals, which were kept on a pantry shelf, usually went out of date before anyone would have more than a bowl. Jesse Lou disdained dry cereal. She referred to it as varmint pellets.

Breakfast served, Jesse and Henri, the maid, whose real name was Henrietta, would have their coffee and breakfast in a nook with a window that overlooked a flower garden in the back yard. Thus, Doc, Emily, and Abby were left to discuss and plan their day.

At age 65, Frank Tynes had cut his practice back to seeing patients for two hours a day in his home office in the back of the house on Monday, Tuesday, and Thursday. He still made house calls whenever he was needed and was determined to perform in that capacity for as long as he could. The new doctor in town, John Phillips, refused to take his medicine bag out of his office.

"It's the way of the future," Frank had told Abby soon after she arrived. "There's coming a day when, if you can't get to a doctor's office, you'll die needing one."

Abby helped plan Doc's day. She scheduled appointments at the office as well as house calls. She handled the billing and often accompanied the doctor on visits. Usually that phase of her job was over by noon. Then she spent time with Emily as a companion for the most part. She learned to play gin rummy and bridge from the older woman. She learned things about the people of the area and the history of the town. Her paid time ended by four o'clock in the evening, but after almost a month in the Tynes' household, she had become more than just an employee. She was more like a daughter to the aging couple. Doc was protective of her and sometimes warned her about local young men who might notice her at church or around town and wish to see her socially. "I've known most all these hometown boys and their families," he would remind her. "And if one is shy or no good, you'd best hear it from me."

Abby was not a young lady to go unnoticed. Several men had already called. But according to Emily, Abby was "particular" when it came to matters of the heart. She should know, because in the few weeks that Abby had been in her home, the older woman had developed a motherly fondness for her. It was Emily who filled the void left by the death of Vivian Rhode a year earlier. It was a loss that Abby was still struggling with. Her writing and her long conversations with Emily were the outlets for her grief.

"I could accept the fact that my dad was ill," she confided one day to Emily. "His death when I was fifteen and my grandmother's three years later were losses I could somehow settle inside myself. But Mom and I worked so hard together after Dad's death to keep the store going. She sent me to business college because she wanted me to be able to take care of myself someday. She held it all together while I was away." Abby cried and apologized for the outpouring of her emotions to Emily, who comforted her and listened.

"We were going to sell the hardware store, move to Charlottesville, and open up a café where she could be the maitre d', and I would play my guitar and sing. That was our dream."

"We all have dreams, Abby," Emily said. "Sometimes they come true, and sometimes they don't. But we must always continue to have them and to speak of them. That's important. When you voice your dream, it is more likely to come true."

"But Mom is gone." Abby fought back tears as she spoke. "She's gone, and so is my...."

Emily reached out and held the young woman's hand in hers. "Life has a way of changing dreams, Abby," she said softly. "You're here, now. There is a reason for everything. Be patient."

It did not take long for Abby to love Doc and Emily Tynes as if they were her own parents. Nor did it take long for her to question the silence that, at times, seemed to separate them.

Dark clouds rolled across the mountains as the wind swept through Abby's bedroom window. The word-filled page she pondered over on the table beside her bed blew over, exposing a blank, lineless page. "Thanks wind," she said sarcastically. "But I can't face another blank page tonight." Abby closed the book. She was tired, and the words just were not coming to her. "Don't force it," she reminded herself.

Distant thunder sounded from somewhere over the mountain. Abby picked up her guitar and sat on the edge of her bed. She strummed a few chords on the old Silvertone instrument before she turned the keys and brought the strings into a tuning she had devised as a young girl. It was based on a more open tuning she had seen used by an old street-corner blues musician in Newport News. With a few adjustments of her own, Abby had created her own chords. "Sweet chords," she called them. They were beautiful, bright and sometimes even sad. Softly, she fingered the notes and strummed the chords to one of her own compositions. And then, as if led into it by her heart's silent urging, she fell into the song that always brought the memory of her parents back to her. She closed her eyes and then in her mind pictured them swaying in the moonlight as she sang so sad and sweetly:

And now when there's moonglow
Way up in the blue
I always remember that moonglow
Gave me you.

Thunder rumbled over the mountain, and Abby opened her eyes and stopped singing. She laid her guitar on the bed and walked over to the window. Flashes of lightning silhouetted the mountains around Buena Vista. Abby closed the window and watched the light-show over the mountains until soft droplets of rain pelted the window panes and blurred her view. Abby touched the cool pane and followed a raindrop with her finger as it drooled down the outside of the glass. She stared up at the mountains and wondered at a mystery which had posed itself soon after her arrival at the Tynes' residence. Questions she had respectfully avoided now loomed in her mind. She had seen photographs on the walls in the den and on Doc's desk in his study. She had walked into the den one afternoon to find Emily staring at a photograph of her husband with a smiling teenaged boy dressed in fishing vests and matching fedoras, posing beside a mountain stream. A string of trout was stretched between them. The photograph was in color, and Abby recalled the hazel blue of the boy's eyes. They were captivating. Emily had told Abby the boy's name was Sherrod. She had smiled when she said it. Doc Tynes had not spoken the boy's name in Abby's presence. She thought that was odd.

One day, she had asked Jesse Lou where Sherrod lived. The rotund woman smiled and said, "Mista' Sherrod live up on the mountain, Missy."

"But doesn't he ever come to visit?" Abby had been at the Tynes' home for several weeks when she asked her question.

Jesse Lou did not answer the question, but looked over at Henri, who was busily ironing table linens while standing in the morning sunlight at the back door.

Henri answered, "Mista Sherrod don't come to visit, lessen it's at night, sometimes."

"But why?" Abby was curious.

"It's jest his way, Missy," Jesse Lou answered and left the kitchen.

Abby turned to Henri, who looked up from her ironing for an instant, then back at her work. But in that instant, Abby knew the house maid knew the answers she desired.

"Henri?" Abby folded her arms as she said the woman's name. She waited.

Finally, Henri spoke. "Me and Jesse Lou been workin' for the doctor and Miz Emily for a mighty long while. And the reason for it, besides the good jobs we do, is that we both knows to mind our own business." She finished creasing a table cloth as she spoke. Then she stopped and set the iron upright, leaned forward on the ironing board, and continued. "Mista Sherrod growed into one fine young man. A special man. But you best hear it from Doc and Miz Emily and not us."

"They haven't said anything about him, Henri." Abby felt dejected. She walked to the kitchen sink and looked out the window into the back yard. "Why all this mystery, Henri?" she finally asked. "I'm living in the same house in which their son was raised, but I haven't met him yet, and everyone tip-toes around his name. I've been on a dozen or more house calls with Doc, and nobody has ever mentioned Sherrod's name out there." Abby's tone was becoming agitated. "I mean, you would think someone would ask how the doctor's son is, or something. Anything. What is he? An axe murderer, or worse?" Abby turned to Henri and waited for a response.

For a moment the thin, little maid said nothing. Then she put her hand to her mouth and emitted a hoarse chuckle. "Lord no, Missy." She regained her composure and continued. "I told you he is special. Not dangerous. Jest different. He was raised here, slept here, and went to school for as long as he had to.

Always a good boy." Henri turned and looked out the back door into the large and well-kept yard. "You see that big ole' magnolia tree there in the yard, Missy?"

Abby walked over and looked out the door. "Yes, I see it."

"Well, when Mista Sherrod was jest a boy, he scurried up that tree like a squirrel and sat up there in the top branches, just a-swayin' in the wind. Jesse Lou done fixed his lunch and says to him, 'How is you gonna eat your soup and sandwich way up in that tree?' And he says to her that she could set it down on the ground and when he finished listenin', he'd come down and eat it. Jesse Lou says to him, 'What you listenin' to?' And he says, 'I'm listening to the tree.' Like it was talkin' to him."

Henri shook her head. "He was mysterious in that way. Always listenin' to somethin' nobody else could hear. And he was a wanderin' soul, too. Always off, galavantin' up in them mountains. Couldn't nobody do nothin 'bout it. It's just his way. Got a wanderin' soul. He was forever bringin' me and Jesse Lou a shiny river stone, or a wild flower. Respectful to the doctor, too. And always has had a special fondness for Miz Emily."

Henri was wound up, and Abby wasn't about to interrupt.

"Why, the older he got, the more time he spent up in the mountains. When he graduated from school, the doctor wanted him to go on to college, but Sherrod couldn't do that. Don't you know, that caused some problems between them two. But Miz Emily, now, she love that boy no matter what. And he come to her even now, when nobody knows he's back."

"Back from where?"

Henri smiled. "Now that's somethin' you gonna have to find out on your own, Missy. I knows a lot. But I cain't tell everythin'."

The thunder and lightning had passed by the time Abby walked downstairs and entered the kitchen. She switched on the light and walked over to the stove, where she turned up the gas and placed the tea kettle on the burner. While the water heated, she walked down the hallway and tapped on the door to Frank Tynes' study.

"The door is open," Doc said as he looked up from the medical book which lay open across his knee. The low lamplight by which he read added to the warm richness of the wood-paneled room.

Abby pushed open the door and smiled. "Tea is on, Doc. Want some?" She stepped into the doorway.

Doc picked up the hard-bound medical book and pulled his chair up to the desk. He plopped the book down on the desktop and removed his glasses. "Think I will, Abby. That's nice of you. Come on in until the whistle blows."

Abby walked over and sat down in an armchair next to the desk. She felt the warmth of the smooth leather upholstery against her body.

Doc turned his chair to face the young woman. "You're doing a fine job, Abby. I don't know what I'd do without you here to keep things straight for me. It all just got to be too much for Em, even with my cutting back as I have. Is she asleep?"

"I don't think so. I saw a light under her bedroom door, and I heard her walking across the floor."

Doc nodded his head. "It's good for her to move around as much as possible. Probably up getting a book to read."

Abby rubbed the armrests nervously with her hands. "That looks like you, Doc." She tried not to be too obvious as she looked at a small framed photo of the doctor and Sherrod. It was placed under the brass desk lamp.

Frank Tynes pressed his lips tightly together and reached across the desktop. He fiddled with the gold-rimmed frame of the photograph and re-adjusted it in its place under the lamp. "Em snapped that photo up in the meadow one summer a few years back." Doc settled back in his chair. He looked at the picture as he spoke. "I believe Sherrod was about eighteen at the time." He looked at the young woman. "The three of us had just come off the mountain."

"Hiking?" Abby asked, hopeful that she could learn more about Sherrod. Doc seemed reflective. "Well, yes, he took us up to see a tree he had discovered."

"A tree?"

Doc smiled and looked back at the photo. "He called it Grandmother. It was a ridiculously large maple that grew up near the headwaters of Noel's Run. The tree was well-protected by the ridges around it and far too difficult a task for someone to take an axe to in the days before it was included in the National Forest. I couldn't believe no one had ever found the tree."

"How do you know they hadn't?"

Doc laughed softly. "Oh, if someone had ever seen that tree, they would have said so. It's massive."

"So, why did he name it Grandmother?" Abby was interested in why someone would name a tree.

Doc flicked a piece of lint off his knee and looked at Abby for a moment before he answered. He opened his hands and shook his head. "That's just Sherrod. You'd have to ask him."

"But, where is…?" Abby stopped her question as the tea kettle whistled in the kitchen.

Doc turned his chair back toward his desk and picked up his book. "Lemon and just a pinch of sugar for me, Abby," he said as he leaned back in his chair with the book on his knee. He found his place in mid-paragraph. But as Abby left the study, Doc's mind wandered back to the meadow and the cabin in the woods on Elephant Mountain.

Before the rain had started that night, Emily Tynes had a premonition. She put down the copy of *The Magnificent Obsession* she was re-reading and arose from her bed to close the bedroom window. A feeling of anticipation came over her as she stood at the window and looked out at the mountains strobed in heavenly lights. The rumble of thunder caused the windows to vibrate in their casings, while the woman sat down in her chair and waited. The wind shuffled the leaves of the walnut tree outside her bedroom window, its strong, sweeping branches bearing close, some would argue too close, to the Tynes' house. It's name was Jonathan. Sherrod had named it when he was a boy, telling Emily never to allow its demise. It would watch over her and protect her. He said Jonathan would always alert him if she needed him to come to her.

The rain came, and Emily waited. Twice she got up and paced nervously across the room. Finally she sat back down and brought the woven afghan from the back of the chair over her legs to ward off the chill. She closed her eyes, and in the midst of the storm that brewed outside her window she imagined the tranquility she knew in the hazel-blue eyes of the young man she called her son. She listened as the wind blew. Wet leaves grazed the roof gutters as a sheet of rain fell hard against the window panes. The stillness of her bedroom heightened her senses, and the hint of a smile crossed her lips when she heard a soft, rhythmic tapping on the window pane.

Emily's eyes were closed, even as a gust of cool, damp air touched her face. She waited for the window to close before she opened her eyes and spoke. "Sherrod," she said almost in a whisper. "I knew you would come." She reached out her hand.

Sherrod Dane smiled and walked over to the woman who had been a mother to him for two decades. He reached down and kissed her cheek. "Hello, Em," he said, kneeling beside her.

The soft fragrance of meadow flowers filled the

bedroom. It was his scent. The smell of his skin. A give-away to his presence. He had brought it home with him that night so long ago, the night Woodrow Marsden had danced with his wife, Lucy. That was when a guarded legend began. A much-guarded legend.

"I told Jonathan that I wished to see you." Emily squeezed Sherrod's hand with both of hers.

The young man smiled. "I think all of the trees knew it. It came to me on a wooded knoll in the Great Smokies down in North Carolina." Sherrod stood up and sat on the edge of the bed. "I came as soon as I heard."

Emily spoke tearfully. "I'm afraid, son."

"What are you afraid of?" Sherrod leaned forward and looked deep into the woman's eyes.

Emily rubbed the afghan on her knees. "I'm afraid for those I leave behind. I'm afraid that things won't be resolved between you and...."

"Listen to me, Em." Sherrod stopped her. "There is one thing left. You know what it is more than I. To voice it is the hardest thing. Because if it's not from your heart, then you are not ready. But don't fear it. Remember, fear is the pathway to greatness."

Emily caressed the young man's cheek with her hand. She forced a smile through her tears. "Did you make that up, or did some wise forest nymph whisper it to you while you slept?"

Sherrod pressed the woman's hand firmly against his cheek. "Grandmother told me that years ago."

"Oh, the maple tree," Emily recalled, her brows lifted.

"She's a wise old girl." Sherrod smiled and winked.

A silent minute went by while Sherrod arose and walked over to the window. Distant lightning flickered across his face as he stood looking at the mountain. He remembered as a child standing at his own bedroom window, staring up at the same mountain. It was his home. His first home. The cabin where he was born. The place where he lived with his mother until the night she left him.

Outside, the wind blew, and raindrops drooled down the window panes. In his mind, Sherrod drifted back to that night long ago and recalled the words his mother had tearfully spoken. "I will never leave you, my beautiful boy," she had promised. "I will just be out for a walk in the woods. Listen with your heart and your mind, and you will hear me always."

"But how will I know it is you, Mama?" he had asked.

"You will know." Her words were labored but reassuring.

Sherrod swallowed hard, then turned and walked over to Emily. "I won't leave you, Em," he said softly. "Don't be afraid."

"Fear is the pathway to greatness." Emily straightened up in her chair and smiled after she had repeated his words. "Let me look at your eyes, Sherrod." The woman reached out her hand and stared into the hazel-blue that had beckoned the mother-love from her heart from the first moment she saw him. The moment soon after his birth in the cabin of another woman. That was where Emily had held Sherrod in her arms for the first time. That was where she saw the truth in his eyes.

"How long will it be, Sherrod?" she asked.

The stillness of the room allowed no escape from the meaning in her whisper.

Sherrod looked deep into the wells of her eyes. A familiar lightness came over him, and his heart fluttered as her spirit revealed itself to his inner mind. Hers was a spirit of goodness and tolerance, an old and wise spirit at the door of light, with but one final task barring the threshold. The sensation of her spirit's revelation surged through his body like a river through his veins, but with it the pain in her bones and the fear she harbored deep within. Moments of her life swirled in a windy tunnel, where dapples of light sparkled on those most precious. Truth spirits began their whisperings. But Sherrod knew when to let go. It was instinctive, an unwritten rule. Spirit stories. Aged lessons. Soulful journeys toward the place of light. It was not his business to go there. But it was in his power to go far enough. With the blink of his eyes and a flutter of his heart, he broke away.

Emily saw it in his eyes when it happened. She felt a sudden weakness in his hands. His eyes closed for a moment, until a deep breath brought him back to her. The clarity of his eyes was brilliant. Honesty lay in the smile that stretched his lips. "You know it is not for me to tell you the day or time, Em," he lightly scolded her, "but to remind you to live each day as if it is your last." He winked and leaned close to the woman. "I'll be close by. Anytime you need me, just say it, and I'll know to come."

Emily embraced Sherrod and then walked with him to the window.

"Tell Doc to come to the mountain when he can." Sherrod opened the window and grasped a thick branch on the walnut tree.

"He's downstairs in his study now."

Sherrod flung his legs over the window seat and leapt into the tree.

"Who is the girl?" he asked as he turned his head back toward the woman.

Emily rested her shoulder against the edge of the window, her arms folded. "Her name is Abby. She's been with us for several weeks now, helping Doc with his calls and paper work."

"What is she to you?"

Emily smiled thoughtfully. "A friend." Her answer was short and honest.

Sherrod understood. He had seen it coming for a long time. Doc was going to see his patients for as long as he could get up and go. But Emily's time to stay at home had come. She could no longer assist her husband on his calls, or even manage the house, let alone the paper work of his practice. It was time for someone to come into the Tynes' home. And it had to be someone besides himself.

A soft knock on the bedroom door drew Sherrod's attention past Emily. He turned and disappeared into the damp blackness of the tree.

Emily closed the window and returned to her

chair. "Come in," she called out as she sat down.

Abby opened the door and entered the room, holding a small wooden tray with two cups of steaming tea. She pushed the door closed with her elbow and walked over to Emily, who was fumbling with the bookmark that had fallen from the pages of her open book.

Abby set the tray down on the bedside table. "I loved that movie," she said.

"Oh? I have never seen the movie." Emily put the marker back in its place and closed the book. "But I wanted to. Didn't it star Rock Hudson and, oh, what's her name?" Emily was frustrated that she could not recall the actress's name.

"Jane Wyman." Abby helped her. She handed Emily her teacup and saucer. "The book is usually better anyway."

Emily placed the book on the corner of the table. "Have you read it, dear?" She blew gently at the rim of her cup and took a tentative sip.

Abby had prepared it the way she preferred, lightly sweetened with a splash of lemon. She placed her cup in its saucer on her lap.

"I read it after I went to see the movie. That might have spoiled it a bit for me." She sat on the edge of the bed. "Is your tea all right?"

Emily stirred her steaming cup with a teaspoon. "It's fine, dear. Just the way I like it."

Abby looked at a white, long-necked vase which contained fresh, yellow jonquils. She was amazed that their fragrance had somehow filled the bedroom.

"The flowers smell so good. It's like a flower garden here next to your bed."

Emily smiled and watched as Abby arose and walked over to the window. "I believe the rain has stopped."

She noticed the girl's bare feet and watched as Abby stopped short of the window and felt the carpet with the ball of her foot.

"Was your window open during the shower? The carpet is wet here." Abby placed her teacup on the window seat and walked into the bathroom. She returned with a hand towel, which she brushed over the carpet and then the window seat. "There," she said when she was finished.

"I'm afraid I was too busy reading before I noticed." Emily felt a tinge of guilt about her lie.

"It's windy tonight," Abby observed as she stared out into the darkness, listening.

Emily watched the beautiful young woman and wondered if perhaps Sherrod had lingered there in the arms of Jonathan just long enough to see her. Perhaps, she thought, he was watching now. If he was, he would certainly notice Abby's perfect shape and countenance. He would describe her hair as midnight. He would heartily approve of her bare feet. And he would see things in the wells of her eyes. "Come and sit with me, Abby." Emily patted the edge of her bed with one hand as she spoke.

The young woman walked across the room and sat down close to Emily.

"There are things I wish to tell you, but I hardly

know where to begin." Emily had grown to trust Abby in the weeks since her arrival. Abby had told her about the death of her father when she was a teenager and how the loss had affected her, her mother, and grandmother. John Rhode had inherited the hardware store from his father and had really never worked at anything else. He grew up assisting his father in the day-to-day operation of the business and had come to know it well. But when his father died at an early age from heart disease, young John realized his mentor possessed something he did not. And that was fortitude. Emmett Rhode had it. It was that attribute that kept him strong, determined, and level-headed through World War I and the Great Depression. Although John was good and honest and smart in the goods he sold, he was also weak in the heart beyond the disease he inherited. He carried far too many credit customers, and in the years after his father died despite the fact that his mother, wife, and daughter helped in the store the business often operated in the red. A second World War was devastating, business-wise. During those years John's mother took to private tutoring at night and Vivian began singing in local clubs for tips, this after helping in the store all day. Abby worked constantly with her father after school and on weekends, until the day she cradled his head in her arms and watched him die on the floor behind the counter.

After that day in 1948, the Rhode women operated the hardware store. Business improved in the post-war years, and by 1952 the store had become

pi
Fc
tha
anc
solc
deci
time
brou‡
the d
it.

"I
Abby
been tc
the Tyn
surroun(
seemed ‡

smiled at me and said that everybody k
but that I'd have to refer to Doc or
So, what about your son? Tell
I can't tip-toe around it any
moment. "I'm a big girl, F
you know that I love yo
me something."
Emily took
to tell a stor
one Abb

...y.

She of al   _ about her son. But
Abby son   _.. icit that it was Emily who harbored
the greatest affection for him. "His picture is on the
walls throughout this house. And yet, he's like a ghost
to me." Abby threw up her hands in exasperation.
"What is it, Emily? What is the secret?" she asked.
"Neither you nor Doc will speak of him. Jesse Lou
walks away at the mention of his name, and Henri's
got me thinking he's some sort of voodoo wild man.

"I mentioned to a waitress named Linda down at
the Piccadilly that I was living here and she seemed
shocked. She guessed I was kin to the family. When I
told her I wasn't, she said, 'Well, I guess you've had a
lot to digest.'

"I asked her if she knew Sherrod, and she just

ew Sherrod,
ou for his story.
ne, please, because
more." Abby waited a
mily. I can take this. And
and Doc. But you have to tell

deep breath and exhaled. It was time
. A story she had never before told. But
Rhode was destined to hear.

Nash Moseley did not like his job at the Hillcrest Dairy Bottle and Distributing Company in Buena Vista. He found it monotonous. And he did not like his co-workers, either. There had already been several disputes with female workers and reprimands from the management. It was always the same. "Leave the ladies alone." That warning should have been impregnated in his mind since he entered puberty. He had certainly heard it enough. But the problem with Nash Moseley was that he never took it to heart. Some would say he had no heart to take it to. The fact was Nash did not care about other people. It was just not in him to concern himself with anything past his own desires and obsessions. He was cruel and calculating, self-absorbed, and prone to violence. He had a confrontational nature and had been that way all his life, despite the fact that he was from a well-thought-of, middle-class family who had strived to offer him every advantage in life. But he would not allow it. He would have been a counselor's nightmare. Anger had eaten into his heart like a cancer, until there was nothing left. There was nothing good in his past, and no ambition for a future. For Nash Moseley there was only the present. Every desire was immediate. Patience did not exist in his world. And the only planning that took place in his devious mind was how to bring everything and anyone he obsessed himself with into his presence and control. Some might say his life was filled with tragedy. But the real tragedies were for those people whose paths had crossed with his. And there were many, most of them women.

Abby Rhode did not know it, but she was Nash Moseley's latest obsession. His sick focus had been on her since the day he saw her sitting in her car at Daniel Glass' service station. He could not get the profile of her face out of his mind. He wanted to smell her skin and hair. His mouth watered at the thought of her touch. Susie Borden, the young blonde who had been with him in the car that day, had become second class to him the instant he saw Abby. He was finished with Susie weeks later. She did not like it, but Nash had to move on. Suzie would not let him breathe. She wanted too much from him. Marriage. He couldn't marry someone like her. She was too young and naive, with high aspirations and no money.

That argument with Susie had been bad. Nobody talked to Nash Moseley like that. Not Susie. Not anybody. She was out of the picture now. Nash whistled as he combed his black hair. When every strand was in place, he sprayed it with hair spray. "Hello, Abby," he lowered his voice and smiled as he watched himself in the mirror. "My name is Nash. Nash Moseley." He practiced as he straightened his tie and buttoned the collar of his white shirt. "How can she resist?" he asked in an over-confident tone while he collected his change and slipped into his dress jacket. He pulled open the third drawer of his chest-of-drawers and rummaged through stacks of smut magazines until he found the Bible that was given to him by the daughter of a tent preacher. A dirty smile creased his lips as he recalled her. "Sweet little Linda," he smirked as he thumped the Bible with his thumb. He shoved the drawer closed and grabbed his car keys. The Timex wind-up clock on the chest showed 10:45 AM. The church was five minutes across town. Nash whistled on his way down the sidewalk to where his black 1956 Bel Air was parked. It was Sunday morning. And Abby Rhode was on his mind.

The steeple bell rang as worshipers filed past Reverend Roy Thomas and out into the front yard of the Buena Vista Baptist Church. The sun was straight up in a cloudless sky when Abby heard the excited voice of a middle-aged woman standing on the sidewalk and peering through the trees toward Elephant Mountain.

"Look up at the rock!" she pointed. "There he is."

Several people heard the woman and cupped their hands over their eyes and gazed up at the mountainside, east of the church.

"I see him," a teenaged girl called out proudly.

"It's Sherrod!" a boy shouted.

Abby looked around her and noticed that for a time, people were looking and pointing.

"It's good he's home again, Emily." A woman with gray hair, dressed in a yellow and white spring suit, squeezed Emily's arm as she passed by.

Emily smiled and nodded. "Thank you, Shirley." She squeezed her husband's arm. "Sherrod wants you to come see him soon, Doc," Emily said as Abby and Doc helped her to the car.

Abby could barely see a figure in a white shirt walk back into the forest from the edge of an outcrop on the side of the mountain. She looked back and saw the preacher wave at the figure up on the mountain, then turn and go back inside the church.

Doc helped his wife into the passenger side of his Park Lane Mercury. "I thought I caught a whiff of him when I came to bed last night." He closed her door and opened the door for Abby to get in the back seat. Then he walked around the car and slid behind the driver's wheel. "He must have come through the window again, right?" Frank Tynes looked over at his wife with a raised eyebrow.

"It's Sherrod's way," was all she would say.

Doc nodded his head, then leaned forward, turned his face, and looked up toward the outcrop.

He watched the crowd of people disperse, some to their vehicles and others along the avenue. "Once word gets around town, there'll be a lot of people up in the meadow this afternoon." He spoke slowly, as if he were thinking at the same time. "Maybe I'll go up to the cabin tomorrow."

"He wants you to come to the grandmother tree." Emily waved at Charles Pauley, who passed by her side of the car.

The man paused and smiled. "I'm going to head up to the meadow after lunch today. Been wanting to see Sherrod for a while." He waved his hand and walked over to his car, where he waited for his wife who was talking to a group of people on the sidewalk.

"How do these people know he'll come to them in the meadow?" Abby was overflowing with curiosity.

Doc looked over at his wife with questioning eyes.

"She knows." Emily anticipated his unvoiced question. She reached back over her left shoulder and offered Abby her gloved hand.

Abby reached out and touched the woman's fingers.

Doc breathed a sigh of relief. "His appearance on the rock up there is his sign that he's back on the mountain and will come to the meadow to see them."

"I want to meet him." Abby was straightforward in her request.

"There's going to be a lot of folks up there today, Abby. You might want to wait and go up with me tomorrow." Doc started the car.

"I'll go then, too, Doc. But today I want to see what this is all about." Abby felt Emily's fingers grip hers as she spoke.

Doc put the car in gear. "Well, young lady, I'll take you up there, but if you ever figure out what it's all about, let me know because I've been wondering about it since 1943."

A tap on Abby's window stopped Doc from letting off the car brakes. He looked back and saw Abby rolling down her window.

"Hello, Abby." A man in a dark suit and stiff black hair bent down and smiled, exposing his tobacco-stained teeth. He smelled of cigarettes and cheap cologne. "My name is Nash Moseley." He reached past Abby's face and extended his hand toward Doc.

Doc felt awkward, but turned in his seat and shook the man's hand.

"Nice to meet you and Mrs. Tynes, sir."

Abby inched herself away from the door.

"What can we do for you, Mr. Moseley?" Doc asked.

"Nash." The man gripped the top rim of the car door with his fingers and peered into the car. "Just call me Nash." He smiled. "I'm kinda new in town and getting to know folks around and about and was wanting to ask if I can come see Abby here and maybe catch a picture show over in Lexington or somewhere."

Frank Tynes took an instant dislike to Nash Moseley from the time the man reached his hand into his car. He also was very aware that as the man talked, he shot quick glances downward toward Abby's cleavage. This was no gentleman. Doc was sure of that.

"Abby?" Doc would not answer for her, although he felt he knew what she would say.

Abby recognized Nash's cold eyes. The uncomfortable feeling she had gotten that day at the service station came over her instantly. She was also aware of his roving eyes and discreetly pulled the hem of her skirt over her knees with one hand as she pressed and fiddled with the top button of her blouse with the other. "I'm settling into my new job with Doctor Tynes right now, Mr. Moseley, and don't have time to go out." She spoke as pleasantly as she could but felt the situation was awkward. "Thank you for asking, though." She smiled nervously.

Nash kept the smile on his face as he was turned down. But Doc saw the corner of his mouth twitch. And he wondered whether it was from disappointment or anger. Of course, he could not know the myriad of vulgar thoughts that leapt through the man's mind as Nash fixed his cold eyes on the dampness that had formed on Abby's delicate neck. He stared at her for long seconds after she spoke and then pushed away from the car and placed his hands in his pockets.

"New place and job. I hear you. I'm there, too. Maybe we'll get together a little later. I'll be seeing you. Probably right here. I like this little church." Nash was trying to be pleasant, but his words were forced, and his effort was thin and obvious.

Abby rolled up the car window.

Doc let off the brake and began pulling away.

"You never know where you might run into 'ole Nash here, Abby," Nash said, walking alongside the car until Doc gave it the gas and left him standing alone on the sidewalk. Nash stood there and watched until the Park Lane turned the corner onto 21st Street and then into the driveway of the Tynes' residence. Then he spit and cursed. He lit a cigarette and took long, deep drags on it while he hurriedly walked past Charles and Shirley Pauley on the way to his car. Once in the car, he angrily tooted his car horn at an elderly couple and revved the motor as they anxiously crossed the avenue in front of him. He rolled down his window and flicked his cigarette butt at their feet as he sped by them up 22nd Street.

Nash Moseley had one thing on his mind that day, and anything or anyone else was nothing to him at all. Nothing.

Sherrod Dane looked down onto the village he had known as a boy. Buena Vista was a town he knew he would never leave. Its people had a special place in his heart. So much of his life was here. And yet, he had ceased walking its streets during daylight hours years ago. There were too many questions. Too many stories. Too many awkward situations and occasional confrontations with well-intentioned people who had no understanding of him or his purpose. But Sherrod understood their confusion. He even understood their sometimes angry outbursts at him. In the beginning he would hear, "Who do you think you are?" Or, "What are you?"

However, Sherrod had never really explained. And after a while, the questions had stopped, and the suspicious faces became friendly again. That was all good, because the truth was complicated. He did not know how to explain what had come over him. But he knew when it had happened. It was the night he fell asleep against the bowl of the beech tree in the front yard of his mother's cabin. That was the night the full moon rose so large over the rooftop. Its glowing brilliance had somehow beckoned him from his slumber and brought him in tune with the true nature of the world around him. Whispers came on the wind that night, and voices, gentle and good, crept from the hearts of the trees like murmurs echoing down a long corridor. He listened intensely and without fear, until the whispers and the voices became one. It spoke his name and asked, "What is it that you want more than anything else?"

His mother's voice was a comfort to him. He could imagine her face, the glint in her eyes, and the warmth of her smile as he contemplated her question. The moonglow that night glistened in his tear-filled eyes as he answered from his heart. "I want to help people who are sick and afraid. I don't want to feel the helplessness that I knew at your bedside."

"Oh, Sherrod," the voice spoke clearly to his mind. "It was my time to become one with all. The fulfillment of my spirit's destiny. My earthly life ended with a new beginning so beautiful and pure. Do not feel guilt for the inevitable. You gave me unconditional love beyond words, and the strength to say goodbye."

Sherrod wept there beside the beech tree that night as his mind voiced his heart. "I miss you always, Mother. That is why I run to the mountain and walk through the house and touch your things, our things. Here, I feel the closeness I never want to lose."

"You must love and respect those who care so deeply for you."

"I do."

"You must always accept the inevitable, because you will see it, good and bad."

"I will," Sherrod promised.

"Then you shall have your wish, Sherrod. But your gift comes with rules and dangers. Rules because of the source from which your power is derived. The dangers will lurk in the shadows of men. You will live in a world where goodness is haunted by temptation and deceit. Beware. You are one among only a few who walk with the gift and know that it is in you to see the light and the darkness of the human spirit. That darkness will seek you out as surely as the lion preys on the lamb. Ask your questions in prayer. The answers will come to you through the wind and water, the blades of grass, and the trees. Love the trees, Sherrod, for they are the oldest living things, and in their voices is the wisdom you seek most."

"Will I hear your voice again, Mother?" the boy asked hopefully.

The great beech tree seemed alive with sensations. Sherrod could feel them through his hands. His body and mind perceived it. "Yes, mine and others. Certain ones of us will speak to you individually. Others, collectively. You will know the names of the most wise, and the language of us all."

"How will I understand? When should I listen? How should I ask?" Sherrod feared he would miss something, or that his imagination was playing tricks on him.

"We speak when there is something to say. We answer when asked." The voice spoke with assurance. "Walk among us with an open heart and listen with your mind. Just as you are now. We are always open to you, but at the time the moon is at its fullest, our voices are strongest."

Sherrod Dane walked away from the beech tree that night a changed person. Gone was his guilt and fear. Worries fell from him like autumn leaves in the wind. He was stronger in mind and spirit. And later that night as he peered into the soul of Woodrow Marsden and lifted the pain from the old man's body, he realized his gift for the first time. From that night in 1943, there had been no turning back, no doubt of his purpose in life. And now, at twenty-eight years of age, Sherrod lived in quiet coexistence with the nature that surrounded him at all times and told him things beyond the grasp of other men.

Sherrod took a deep breath of cool air into his lungs and exhaled it. He watched for a moment as cars and trucks moved along the streets and avenues of Buena Vista. He listened to the church bell as it rang out. Then he turned and walked back into the shadows of the forest he knew so well. The walk to the meadow would not take long.

Abby was excited. Finally, she would meet the young man whose mysterious image had somehow consumed her thoughts since soon after her arrival in Buena Vista. The young man whose life had been concealed, even protected, by those who knew him best.

Emily Tynes had finally offered her some explanation of Sherrod. She had referred to him as "special" and "gifted," and "a Godsend." Powers were mentioned though not explained.

Abby knew that Emily adored Sherrod. She knew about the nighttime visits and how he usually avoided the front door of the house. Sherrod's window entries seemed adventurous and free-spirited to her. The fact that he avoided venturing into the village during the daylight hours was becoming more understandable to her as she pieced together the story of his life through photographs of him in family albums and conversations with Emily.

The moon was full on the night Sherrod was born in a cabin on Elephant mountain. It was April, 1930. Emily always referred to him as her son. But he was really the son of Laura Dane, a reclusive but talented woman who had chosen a life of solitude after the death of her husband. Flavius Dane, a well-to-do merchant seaman, had passed through Buena Vista on a land-purchasing journey in the early 1920s. He had been captivated with the beauty of the highland meadow and the heavily forested mountain range that bordered the eastern side of town. Flavius bought the meadow and four hundred acres of a mountain range deemed impossible to farm. But farming was not his forte. The rolling beauty of the blue-green mountains simply reminded him of ocean swells. The vastness of the Blue Ridge Mountains to the east and the Appalachians to the west fascinated the man who had lived most of his life at sea.

He built his cabin using great chestnut logs he felled from the forest and hued with his own hands. Dane was a natural craftsman and built his cabin in a cradle in the mountain, among great oaks and beech trees. He traveled to Buckingham County and brought back truckloads of slate for its roof. He fashioned his house with a wrap-around deck so that he could walk around it and hear the thud of his boot heels, a sound he loved to hear upon the deck boards of his ships.

Flavius filled his cabin with comfortable furniture made by local artisans. He bought the paintings of local artists and adorned the walls with colorful depictions of mountains, waterfalls, native animals, and trout streams. He traveled into the Great Smokies and brought back beautifully detailed Cherokee blankets; some covered the beds and others were used as throws.

Flavius had lived alone in his cabin for a year, until the call of the sea beckoned. At dawn on the day he left, he stood on the outcrop overlooking the village and watched the lights come on, one-by-one, in the houses far below. He had come to know many of the townspeople. He admired their heartiness and simple ways. He loved the silence at dawn in the mountains. A lone tom turkey gobbled in the distance, and a warm breeze rose from the valley, coaxing the treetops in long waves and sudden ripples. Flavius knew he would someday take a wife and settle here for good.

Three years later, he sold his ships on the southeast coast and made his way back to his cabin on Elephant Mountain. At his side was Laura, a beautiful, young singer-guitarist from Newport News, who had believed his promises and waited for his return.

They married in the highland meadow on a spring morning. Laura's golden hair lifted in the breeze as she played her guitar and sang songs of love to her husband. The preacher and the few guests who were there would never forget the happiness in the meadow that day.

Emily and Frank Tynes had been there. That is how Emily could tell the story. But it was not all such a happy story. Although the Danes lived in their cabin on the mountain for five years, they never really became a part of the community. Flavius was often away on business. When he was home, he and Laura would sometimes attend church services or an occasional social function. But few lasting connections were made, except perhaps with some of the children of the town. They were the ones who came to the meadow and listened to Laura sing and play her guitar. They and the childless Tynes, Emily and Frank. Woodrow and Lucy Marsden would often bring their horse and buggy up to the meadow and give the children rides. That was a happy time, when songs and laughter filled the hillsides. Laura reveled in the attention and had a true fondness for the children. Flavius was usually away, but when he was there, he seemed proud of his wife. And yet, there was a distance between the two. Words unspoken. Glances avoided.

Emily was aware of it, even if no one else seemed to be. So one day she asked, and with a tearful reply, Laura said, "I cannot give him the ocean. And he cannot give me what my heart cries out for."

Perhaps it was the things unsaid or private implications known to but two hearts and the chestnut walls of the cabin on the mountain that brought an end to their lives together. It was on a warm August morning in 1929 when Flavius Dane clutched his chest and drew his last breath as his young wife wept at his side. As sure as God has wit, life has its ironies. Sometimes these are subtle and private—a quiet and humbling joke. And sometimes not. The people around us can see and laugh or shake their heads. But few knew Laura Dane. And the one who most understood the irony of her life would soon realize her own irony.

After the death of her husband, Laura lived by herself on the mountain. But she was not alone. The children of Buena Vista still came to the meadow to listen to her songs. They loved her. Woodrow and

Lucy practically adopted her. But Emily became her dearest friend. And it was Emily who held her hand and comforted her and aided Doc on that full-moon night the following spring, when Laura gave birth to Sherrod in the cabin that Flavius had built. The bond of true friendship has a mystifying strength. When tested time and again, it draws tighter, secure even in death. A part of someone's heart died that night amid the pain and joy of Sherrod Dane's birth. Or was it a test of friendship?

Abby held a white short-sleeved blouse up to her neck and looked in the mirror at her image. She crinkled her nose and replaced the blouse with a lightweight mint-colored turtleneck. "Too hot," she said, throwing the turtleneck on the bed. She unbuttoned the white blouse, tossed the hanger on the bed and put it on. She liked how the short-waist blouse fell just below the belt loops of her khaki capri pants, allowing the slimness of her waist to be accentuated. "That's it," she said aloud. She sat on the bed and put on her white cloth sneakers.

A minute later, she tapped on Emily's bedroom door and stepped in. "How do I look?" she asked with girlish excitement.

Emily looked across the room at the young woman and smiled. "Cute as a button, dear." The older woman stepped away from the window and sat down in her chair. "Doc has started the old truck. You'd better get going."

Abby could hear the truck's motor running steady and low. "Will there really be a lot of people up there, Em?"

Emily raised her eyebrows. She could sense Abby's nervousness. It reminded her of a school girl going out on her first date.

"I would think there will be a fair crowd. He's been away for a few weeks."

Abby started out the door but stopped and bit the inside of her bottom lip before she asked softly. "Do you think he will notice me?"

Emily looked at the beautiful girl standing in the doorway for only a moment before she answered. "He won't be able to take his eyes off you."

Abby's face lit up. "What will I say?"

"You won't have to say anything. Just be yourself."

"Thanks, Em. Is there anything I can get for you before we go?"

Emily shook her head. "Enjoy your trip to the meadow. And tell me all about it when you get home."

Abby smiled, turned and closed the door behind her.

Emily listened as Abby hurried down the stairs. She heard the back door close and then the sound of the truck backing out of the garage. The phone rang as Doc pulled the truck onto the avenue. Emily picked up the receiver on the third ring. "Hello, Doctor Tynes' residence. This is Mrs. Tynes. Can I help you?"

For a few seconds there was silence. And then just as Emily was about to repeat herself, the caller hung up.

"How do they come to him, Doc?" Abby asked her question while rolling down her window and adjusting the side vent so that the warm afternoon air would not blow in her face.

Frank Tynes reached down and pulled the vent handle, adjusting it for a quiet flow of air. "They drive up Indian Gap Run and park along the trace. Then they walk up a path the rest of the way to the meadow."

"What about folks who can't walk that far?"

Doc smiled at Abby's inquisitiveness. "They run," he chuckled.

"Doc." Abby shook her head.

"I usually know about those people, Abby. We just make other arrangements."

"So you are in on this." Abby made her statement and waited for Doc to come clean.

Doc scratched the side of his head and glanced at his passenger. His expression was serious. "Abby, I'm a medical doctor, and I believe in the science of medicine, rest, and therapy. I give preventive advice. In most cases, I can diagnose and be pretty darn accurate. If a patient listens to me and adheres to my advice, they usually get better. If I'm stumped, there are colleagues

I can call. If a patient is not responding to treatment, I'll try something else or sometimes send them to a specialist." The doctor paused for a moment and cleared his throat. "And then there are some things, some ailments that are just out of my realm."

Abby looked over at the doctor. She had formed a great respect for this man who had brought her into his home and practice. She had gone out many times with him on house calls and had witnessed the respect the community had for him. He was quiet, thoughtful, and good. She knew he loved Emily, and yet there were times when silences swelled between them. She felt that he loved Sherrod also, but a guarded silence cloaked the man when his name was mentioned. For weeks Abby had been confused. But now she was putting it together in her mind. Today she would know for sure.

"But not out of his realm." Abby's words were not intended as a question.

Doc turned up Indian Gap trace and allowed the truck to creep along the rut-filled dirt road. "I've seen him do things, marvelous things, since he was thirteen years old. As a doctor of medicine, I can't explain a lot of what I've seen him do, or the things I've been told. I don't think scientists can explain it either. I don't expect them to. But it's as natural to Sherrod as breathing. I don't know if the cures or the healing are through his faith or their faith or what. I just know it happens, and it's through him, somehow. I guess maybe I've just learned to…." Doc pulled the truck to the side of the road.

Abby spoke what was on his lips. "Accept it."

Doc pressed his lips together and then slowly nodded his head. "Yes, Abby. I've come to accept it." The man seemed relieved.

Abby reached over and patted his hand. "Will you come to the meadow with me, Doc?"

Doc let go of the steering wheel and squeezed the young woman's fingers with his right hand. "We stay out of each other's examining rooms," he smiled. "When it's over, he knows where I'll be. You follow him up to the cabin, okay?"

"All right." Abby opened the truck door. "How do I get there?" She stepped out of the truck as a car passed slowly by.

Doc waved at the driver and pointed up the road. "Over the hill, beyond those cars. There's a path up into the forest on your right. Just follow the people."

Abby looked up the dirt road. She closed the truck door. "Where will you be?" she asked.

"I won't be far away. Not far at all." He watched Abby walk up the road and disappear over the rise. Then he got out of the truck and walked into the woods.

In the months since Nash Moseley had come to Buena Vista, he had heard Sherrod Dane's name mentioned only a few times. But on two occasions, his name was linked to miraculous events. Once by a middle-aged female employee at the bottle company, who swore Sherrod had healed her mother of a severe kidney infection that was threatening her life with no more than a touch of his hand. The other by Dan Glass over at the service station, when Nash overheard him telling Will Barnes about a young mother who had accidently slammed her young son's hand in a car door. Dan said he had heard her shrill calls for help from across the parking lot of the Knight's General Store and rushed to her aid. He found the woman frantically trying to open the car door, which was jammed. The screaming child's hand was wedged up to his wrist in the door when Dan arrived. He attempted to open the jammed door. The boy's hand came free on Dan's third attempt, and both the mother and Dan were horrified at the severity of the boy's injury. All five of the boy's fingers were broken. Two fingers were out of their joints, and a deep gash made by the door's lock was bleeding profusely. Dan wrapped the boy's hand in his handkerchief, consoled the mother and child for a minute, then rushed into the store to call Doc Tynes, only to learn that he was out making house calls. Dan then grabbed a new dish towel off the store shelf and filled it with ice from the soda cooler. He ran back out to the frantic mother and child and wrapped the boy's hand in the cold compress. He explained that the doctor was out and there was only one man nearby who could help them.

The young woman put her trust in Dan and drove the three of them up Indian Gap trace, where she parked the car and followed Dan as he carried the whimpering youth in his arms up a path through the trees and across the meadow. Dan had called out to Sherrod a few times before he stopped at the edge of the forest, but he had not called loudly. And yet as he knelt and placed the boy in the cool, long grass beneath a large oak tree, a young man stepped out of the shadows.

Sherrod nodded his head at Dan and glanced at the face of the worried and out-of-breath mother. "What's your name?" he asked the boy in a soothing voice while kneeling on both knees in the grass beside him.

"Ronnie," the boy answered, his eyes intent on Sherrod's face.

Sherrod looked into the boy's eyes and smiled. Carefully, he lifted the boy's wounded hand and removed the compress, exposing the jagged gash and broken fingers.

"There is a great crested flycatcher in my woods this summer, Ronnie." He spoke softly while removing a bottle of what looked like water from a satchel he carried across his shoulder. "Wheep," he called softly as he poured the warm liquid over the boy's hand. "Listen, and you can hear it answer me from the crevice of a tree where it hides."

The boy had stopped his whimpering. He was mesmerized, his body still.

Dan and the boy's mother watched in silence as Sherrod washed away the boy's blood. They noticed as he laid his palm over the clean wound and pressed it, his eyes never leaving the boy's gaze. "Do you hear it, Ronnie?" He removed his palm from the wound revealing the boy's smooth, unbroken skin where the gash had been.

The mother gasped and held her hands to her lips. Dan waited.

"Wheep!" Sherrod whistled loud and clearly. "He's left the shade of his hiding place now and is coming to see you." Sherrod spoke while holding Ronnie's broken and misshaped fingers in the warmth of his own hands. "Can you hear the flycatcher, Ronnie?" he asked again.

The boy's eyes lit up. "He's behind you," he whispered.

Sherrod smiled and let go of the boy's hand. A flutter of wings came low over their heads, and Dan looked up to see the yellow belly and white wing bars of the bird which loudly announced its presence.

The boy sat up and raised his wounded hand in the air. That was when Dan and the boy's mother saw that his once broken fingers were straight again. His wound had been healed.

Nash Moseley had become intrigued by Dan's story that day at the service station, and although he was an uninvited listener, he imposed himself by asking Dan Glass if he really believed such a thing had happened.

The older man did not like the implication or Nash's imposition and answered flatly. "It doesn't matter what I or you or anyone believes when it comes to Sherrod Dane. But I know what I've seen, and it's no hoax."

Dan and Will had then walked out the door and continued their conversation outside, leaving Nash alone with his thoughts. And they were dark thoughts, beyond those which normally dwell in the hearts and minds of envious people. But there was nothing normal about Nash. His envy could turn to loathing in an instant.

So now there were two reasons why Nash turned onto Indian Gap trace and passed by Doc Tynes' parked truck that Sunday afternoon. One was to pursue his sick lust for Abby. And the other was to come face-to-face with Sherrod Dane, the mysterious healer of the mountains. The man who, in Nash's dark heart, was a hoax and, somehow, a threat to him.

Nash parked his car and then watched in his rearview mirror while Abby walked up the road and joined a small group of people from the church as they stepped onto the winding path that led into the woods. Nash took a long drag on his cigarette, then opened the car door and stepped out. He threw his cigarette butt into the middle of the road, blew a long stream of smoke after it, then slammed the car door shut and walked toward the path. Halfway to the meadow, he leaned against a maple tree, wheezing. Tiny mosquitoes buzzed in the stillness around his head. A thin trickle of sweat coursed its way down his right temple. He cursed to himself and lit another cigarette.

A man and woman passed by him with their teenaged daughter. The man spoke politely, but Nash did not acknowledge him. Instead, he watched the man's daughter as she walked beside her mother up the hill.

He undressed the girl with his cruel eyes. He spat and licked his lips. He smiled as the vision of his vulgar imagination played in his mind's eye.

When Abby stepped from the shade of the forest and into the mid-afternoon sunlight, she found herself in awe of the meadow that lay before her. A myriad of colors danced in the warm breeze and dazzled her eyes. Green grass and clover were the backdrops to splashes of colorful islands of yellow, lavender, and red wild flowers. Buttercups, black-eyed Susans and pussytoes grew sporadically as if a great hand had strewn them from the sky. An orchard of fruit trees grew along the eastern slope of the meadow. Granite boulders rose from the rich ground in places like the shells of partially hidden turtles.

Boys and girls ran up the gray-black boulders and called to each other. The meadow was alive with the flutter of butterfly wings and the constant drone of honeybees. Birds flitted in and out of the grasses and flowers, and the forest on all sides echoed with their songs. A tiny bluebird lit upon the yellow flower-head of a gray goldenrod, just long enough for Abby to be amazed at its brilliant plumage. She watched as the little bird swooped low across the meadow and then up into the leafy shade of a dogwood tree at the edge of the woods.

Abby followed the course of the people across the meadow. She approached the gathering place slowly, distancing herself from her friends.

The place resembled a natural amphitheater, a shallow bowl along the western edge of the meadow, where towering hardwood trees stood like protecting gods between the light of the field and the dappled mystery of what lay behind them.

Abby watched as people carefully found places to sit among the clover and wild flowers. Even the children were careful not to crush a petal in this place. Abby counted sixty-four people when, at last, all were seated in the shade of the trees. Some people sat upon the cool grass and clover, while others had brought blankets. One very young couple sat out in front and closer to the forest edge than anyone else. In the arms of the young mother was a baby wrapped in a thin, patched quilt. The woman swayed back and forth with the child at her breast. Her eyes were dark and sunken. Her husband quietly rubbed her back and whispered close to her ear.

Abby sat apart from the rest of the people, but watched as they settled in and waited, their eyes toward the trees. A silence came over them as the minutes passed. Children lay with their heads in their mother's or father's laps. No one spoke for a while.

The shadow of a cloud crept across the meadow and caught Abby's attention. Then she saw the man she recognized as Nash Moseley walking toward her. Cigarette smoke seeped from his mouth when he made eye contact with her and grinned. She was noticeably alarmed and got up and moved closer to her friends.

Nash noticed her quickness to avoid him. Perturbed, he sat on a flat rock at the rear of the gathering. He huffed and flicked his cigarette butt into the lush green clover. A grasshopper lit on his pant leg. Instead of ignoring it or brushing it off with his hand, he crushed its head between his tobacco-stained forefinger and thumb. He dropped the grasshopper beside his foot and mashed it into the grass with the heel of his shoe. It meant nothing to him. He started counting the people, but lost interest before he could finish. He looked at his watch and then stared at the back of Abby's head. She had made it obvious that she did not want to have anything to do with him. But that was not a deterrent for Nash. It never had been.

Abby extended her arms behind her and leaned back. The thick clover felt cool between her fingers. There was not a cloud in the sky now. She closed her eyes and, for an instant, she saw her mother and father swaying in the moonlight at her bedroom window. She imagined her mother's voice on that night long ago. So delicate. She remembered the song. Every word of it.

The wind shifted. Abby felt it on her face. The smell of meadow flowers rode on its gentle wave from the woods.

"He's coming. I see him." A boy sat up and pointed his finger.

Abby opened her eyes and looked past the shadow of the trees. She watched and waited. Her heart was beating fast. Dapples of sunlight through the forest canopy. A movement in sync with nature. Silence. Abby swallowed and blinked her eyes. In that moment, he appeared. Her heart fluttered as the handsome young man stepped from the shadows of his realm.

"Sherrod." A young girl sitting near Abby spoke his name.

A smile formed across Sherrod's tanned face. He nodded and looked at the girl. His hazel-blue eyes were intense, yet kind. Without a word, he removed a satchel from his shoulder and placed it at the base of an ancient white oak. Water trickled out of the ground next to the tree, collected in a natural depression, and then spilled into a narrow run before it disappeared beneath the exposed roots of a nearby beech tree.

Sherrod stooped and immersed his hands in the cool water. He closed his eyes for a moment and then stood up and looked out among the people.

Abby had studied the photographs of Sherrod Dane on the walls and shelves and in the photo albums at the home of his adoptive parents. Through those photographs she had seen him change from a boy to a man. But the person she saw emerge from the forest that day was beyond the still life of a photograph and even her imagined perception of one she somehow felt destined to know.

Finally, he was standing here before her, as alive as the world around him. In silent moments she studied him. He was tall and as muscular as one would expect a man of nature to be. His hair was as blonde as corn silk and swept back. He wore it much longer than the men of his day, with strands of it wisping at his shoulders. His forehead and facial features were well-defined. Abby thought his nose and lips were perfect. His jawline was less than square, yet no one would have described him as long in the face. Broad shoulders and a thin waist implied strength and vigor. Abby thought he looked younger than his years physically, and yet there was something about him that went beyond worldly years. There was an aura of wisdom emanating from him. His clothes were simple, but fitting: A long-sleeve white linen shirt rolled up to his elbows, khaki pants, a belt, and beautifully beaded moccasins. He wore no jewelry. He was the most handsome man Abby thought she had ever seen.

When Sherrod finally spoke, his voice was strong yet soothing. "I have been away from the mountain for too long, my friends. Its call to my heart was strong, and I am glad to be home again." Sherrod stayed close to the oak tree as he spoke. "I will not leave you for a while."

"Where did you go?" a boy asked while chewing on a clover stem.

"I went where I was needed." Sherrod smiled.

"Were the people kind to you?" another child asked.

"The kind-hearted are always kind."

"Did you heal and save anybody?" Nash Moseley's question was loud and challenging. He smirked when he posed it, proud of his brashness.

Abby did not join the crowd of people as they turned around angrily. Instead, she kept her eyes on Sherrod.

Two young men rose to their feet and faced Nash.

Sherrod asked them to sit down, and they did. Then he answered calmly. "I did not heal anyone who could not heal themselves."

Nash snickered. "Well, shucks, man. I thought you could walk on water." He stood up and held up his hand. "I mean, look here, man. I got a wart on the side of my thumb, here." He shook his hand in the air. "Can you do warts?"

Several men rushed back to confront Nash, but he did not mind a threat. He reveled in his own belligerence. He craved what most good men would see as unnecessary confrontation. He needed to belittle others. Deep inside he needed to do it. It made him feel bigger and better than he was. This was part of his sickness.

But Nash misjudged the people he had followed into the meadow that day. He thought they were just church-going "do-gooders." Their meekness was their weakness, in his mind. Small-town. Small minds. He could not have been more wrong about them. Each one had a reason to be in the meadow that day. Each one had formed a bond with Sherrod stronger than the shallow mind of Nash Moseley could have ever comprehended. Their devotion to this man of nature, their mysterious healer, was the source of their silence about him to outsiders. Sherrod was one of them, a native son, special among them in a way which garnered him their protection — a protection of silence which kept away the headline seekers, the curious, and the nay-sayers bent on proving him a fraud.

Through his intrusive nature, Nash had heard trickles of conversations about Sherrod. Whispers among his co-workers at the bottle company. "Is he back on the mountain?" someone would ask. Or, "Are you going to the meadow?"

Nash had learned that Sherrod was the adopted son of Doctor Frank and Emily Tynes. He had heard of his curious ability to commune with nature, with trees in particular. But the healing was the part that both intrigued and angered him. Nash's curiosity was perhaps normal, whereas the anger that fed his jealousy and contempt was not. That anger sprang from a dangerous seed, a seed planted long ago that would thrive in the darkness of his heart and rule him as a master to a slave. Nash Moseley did not belong in the meadow that day. He knew it, as did the people around him. But the voice that guided him from within was strong. It coaxed his vulgar desire for Abby and urged his disrespect for every good thing. It forced him into the meadow that summer day with a shield of arrogance surrounding him and the confidence that a reckoning was at hand. For a reason even he could not fully comprehend, Nash wanted to somehow lower Sherrod Dane in the eyes of the people of Buena Vista. But what he did not know was that there had been others before him. Dark hearts and tempters, whose evil designs had been revealed through their own eyes. All had failed, because none had known the power they came up against in Sherrod.

Angry hands pulled Nash to his feet, while a murmur moved through the gathering.

"Leave here," a man demanded. Fists clenched in anger as Nash jerked away.

Another man shouted, "Go away!"

"Idiots!" Nash smirked as he took a step back.

Suddenly men stepped away, and Nash came face-to-face with Sherrod.

"Let him stay." The young man spoke calmly, while he walked directly up to Nash. "Go and sit down, friends," Sherrod instructed the men. "Let me speak to this man alone."

Nash watched as the men quietly dispersed. "You really got a hold on 'em, don't you?" He posed his question while looking at the gathering of people and then up at the sky. Anything to avoid eye contact.

In an instant Sherrod had seen enough in Nash's eyes to know what drove the man. He spoke quietly, but with authority. "Stay if you wish. But after today, do not step a foot into this meadow."

Nash smiled nervously. "I'm Nash Moseley, and you can bet that I will do as I please."

Sherrod studied the man's face as he spoke. He saw the sweat bead on his forehead and above his upper lip and the twitches at the corners of his mouth. He could sense Nash's discomfort.

"Stay if it pleases you. It makes no difference to me." Sherrod turned and walked back through the gathering toward the oak tree.

Nash shrugged his shoulders and sat down on the flat rock. His nerves were rattled, and he did not like that. He was angry at the fact that his brief encounter with Sherrod had done that to him. He was confused as to why he could not look the man in the eye. But he was curious, so he watched and waited in silence.

When Sherrod reached the oak tree, he placed his

hands on its trunk and, closing his eyes, leaned his forehead against it. No one moved or talked during the moments he stood there, still and quiet.

Abby wondered if he was praying. Something. Some unseen communication was taking place. She knew it. She could feel it, as if she were connected to it in some way.

When Sherrod opened his eyes, he stepped away from the tree and turned to the people. He smiled and motioned to the young couple sitting closest to him to come forward.

Abby watched the young mother offer her whimpering baby to him. Sherrod cradled the baby in his arms, then spoke to the woman in a gentle tone. "How long has this child cried through the night?" he asked while massaging the baby's stomach.

"Four months now," the woman answered.

Sherrod looked into her eyes and felt her weakness and helplessness. She was gaunt, with shadows around her eyes. He looked over at her husband and read the worry on his face. "Don't fear for your child," he assured them. "He has colic." Sherrod then inhaled a breath of air and lowered his mouth to the infant's lips, where he gently exhaled.

The baby immediately quieted and closed his eyes.

Sherrod gave the child back to his mother. "The three of you will sleep tonight," he said while kneeling down and reaching into his satchel. He brought out a small cloth bag and handed it to the father. "Make a tea of these leaves and give it to your child when he awakens." He touched the young man on his shoulder. "He will be fine."

The young man shook Sherrod's hand and thanked him. Then he and his wife and child returned to their place in the cool grass.

Sherrod smiled. "There is someone here with the hiccups. Come."

A middle-aged woman held her fingers to her lips as she stood up and walked over to Sherrod.

"Hello, Sarah." He greeted her warmly and reached into his satchel. He brought out a bag of seeds. "How long have they bothered you?"

Sarah seemed embarrassed. "Night and day for two weeks."

Sherrod filled her palm with seeds. "Chew these now and by the time you sit back down, you will be free of your hiccups."

The woman chewed the seeds, then turned and walked back to her place beside her husband. She laughed when she sat down and said aloud, "They're gone!"

"I can't sleep," an old man called from his seat in the grass. "What can you do, Sherrod?"

Sherrod walked over to the man. "Take the dried pine needles from the trees in your yard, Wallace. Crush them in a bowl and then light them with a match. Allow them to burn for a minute, then blow out the flame. Put the bowl with the smoking embers on your bedside table and they will fill your room with a delightful fragrance. Inhale it and you will sleep."

Sherrod smiled and patted his stomach. "Do not

eat so much for supper, Wallace. And take a long walk each day. That will also help."

Over the next hour, Sherrod either cured or gave remedies for everything from acne to morning sickness. He massaged an old woman's temples and alleviated her pain from a migraine headache. Then he suggested a tea to thwart its return. One man, whose heart beat out of rhythm, was placed into a deep sleep. While he lay there, Sherrod laid a hand on his chest and closed his eyes. When the man awoke, his heart was back in rhythm.

Abby watched and listened. She noticed every move Sherrod made. She sensed his calmness. His goodness. No wonder the people loved and protected him. No wonder they sheltered him from the outside world and the exploitations of strangers. He was one of their own. But special in a way that set him apart.

Now Abby could understand more of his mystery. She could not imagine him holding a job in town or walking the streets in the daylight or even sitting in a church. He belonged to the nature around him. The trees and plants. The mountains, streams, and rivers. The meadow. For whatever reason, Sherrod had been given a gift, and Abby knew in her heart, just as all those who had put their trust in him, that the source of that gift was God. The knowledge of remedies was one thing. But the touching and healing, and the ability to see things by gazing into one's eyes, were beyond the common.

In the late afternoon an old, ragged man crossed

the meadow and, with the aid of a cane, walked past the gathering of people.

Abby saw him walking unsteadily toward Sherrod. His shoulders were hunched, and his face wrinkled and drawn, with sunken cheeks and eyes. No one seemed to know him, nor did they speak to him. The man kept his eyes on the ground, not looking at the people or even at Sherrod, who waited patiently next to the oak tree.

"What can I do?" Sherrod asked when the man finally stopped in front of him, his head bowed.

A strange moment of silence passed before the man raised his head and looked at Sherrod. "Save me," he begged pathetically. "Save me, Sherrod Dane."

In the time it took him to speak, Sherrod felt the old man's pain and saw him wretched and full of sin. The scent of death came to Sherrod's nostrils, and he winced and turned his head. "I cannot save you, old man," he said.

"But if you have the power to heal, then you must...."

Sherrod halted the man's speech by raising his hand and speaking. "It is not for me to do."

The old man lowered his head for a moment.

Abby could see his gnarled hands tremble as he tightened his jaw and glared up at Sherrod.

"What kind of man are you? You will not cleanse an old man of his sins?" He shook the handle of his cane toward Sherrod's face as he questioned him. There was anger in his voice.

But Sherrod did not flinch. There was no surprise

or fear in his expression when he responded. "The kind who knows a tempter when he sees one." He nodded his head toward the hillside where Nash was standing alone. "Go and stand in the shadow of the dark heart, old man. That is where you belong. Not here, in the midst of these good people. You have tried me and failed." He turned away from the old man then, bent down and picked up his satchel.

Abby saw the hint of a wicked smile form in the corner of the old man's mouth as he turned and walked away. No one spoke to him, and although he acknowledged Nash with a quiet nod of his head, he avoided contact with him. Instead, he trudged up the hill and back across the meadow. His long shadow preceded him through the clover.

Sherrod brought the strap of his satchel over his head and secured it on his shoulder.

The people stood up when he turned back toward them. "Tell those who need my help where they can find me." He touched the oak tree with one hand as he spoke. "Tell those who are too ill to make the trip here that I will come to them when the stars awaken."

A gray-haired man brought a large basket over to Sherrod. Abby could see that it was packed with bread, cheese, and fruit.

"Here is a list of the shut-ins, Sherrod." The man handed the basket to Sherrod and slipped a folded paper between a loaf of bread and an apple.

Sherrod smiled and took the man's offering. "I will see to them, Charles. Tell them that."

Abby stood and looked up the hill. Nash was staring

at her. His audacity was unnerving. A chill ran up her spine. There was something so evil about him. She had seen it the day she first came to town, that day at Dan Glass' service station, when Nash drove his black car slowly by her and stared. In those seconds, she had felt vulnerable. Threatened. And then when he had accosted her after church, she had felt his eyes exploring her. Instinctively, Abby knew Nash was a dangerous man. She could not walk back across the meadow. Not even surrounded by her friends. He would approach her, she knew it. And it frightened her.

Nash started down the hill toward her, and she turned intentionally and walked over to where Sherrod was speaking with the man who had given him the food basket. Her heart was racing when Charles Pauley noticed her approach. He reached out his hand, touching her elbow. "Well, hello, young lady," he said with a smile. "I see you found the meadow."

Abby could feel her heart pounding in her throat. She smiled nervously and glanced up the hill.

Instantly, Sherrod followed her glance with his sharp eyes and met the uneasy stare of Nash, who stopped immediately, turned, and walked in the opposite direction.

Abby saw him turn away and breathed a sigh of relief.

Charles Pauley noticed something more than an uneasiness in Abby's demeanor and followed her eyes toward the hillside. A moment later, he cleared his throat. "Sherrod," he said, "I guess you've already met Abby, here." He gently pulled Abby closer in.

Sherrod smiled and looked directly into Abby's eyes. "No, I'm afraid not. But Em has told me about her."

Abby reached out her hand and felt Sherrod squeeze her fingers. "Hello, Sherrod," she said while trying to regain her composure. She hoped her nervousness was not overly noticeable. But the truth was, she was bursting inside with excitement. Finally, after weeks of anticipation, she was meeting Sherrod Dane. Finally, she had heard the voice of the young man in the photographs. The man whose very name brought smiles and unspoken reveries to the faces and minds of practically everyone she had come to know. The mystery protected by the people of Buena Vista. Their wonderful secret. Her long-awaited discovery.

Abby looked into Sherrod's hazel-blue eyes and felt an openness within her that she had never before experienced. There was no need for caution. In mere seconds, she felt a oneness with him. For a moment, the sadness over the loss of her parents seemed distant, and the fear of Nash Moseley was all but forgotten.

Charles Pauley cleared his throat again, and Abby blinked her eyes. But by then a spell of enchantment had been cast. Abby felt it the moment it occurred. Sherrod knew it when he looked into her eyes. The image was clear. This was the girl whose teardrops he had seen glistening in moonglow on the night his life had changed. The child had become a woman. She was the one he had waited for. And her name was Abby.

"Old Doc sure has been braggin' on this gal,

Sherrod." Charles' voice broke a silence both Sherrod and Abby wanted to last.

Abby blushed at the compliment.

Sherrod could not take his eyes off her. "Em is very enamored with her also." Sherrod recalled the night Emily had told him of the young woman who had come to their home. He remembered the lightness of her spirit when she mentioned Abby's name.

"Haven't seen Emily and Doc for a while." Charles sounded concerned. "How is she?"

Abby knew the answer to Charles Pauley's question. But she waited for Sherrod to answer.

"Her body is growing weaker all the time, Charles. But her mind and heart are still strong."

Charles sighed and shook his head. "God bless her," he said thoughtfully. "I know she's glad you're back home." He patted the younger man on the arm.

Sherrod smiled. "Thanks, Charles."

"Can I take you home, Abby?" Charles' offer broke a moment of shared sadness.

Abby looked at Sherrod, then smiled back at Charles. "Oh, no thanks, Mr. Pauley. I'll ride back with Doc. He's up at Sherrod's place now."

The older man raised his eyebrows and smiled. "Good then. You tell the doctor I said howdy." Charles shook Sherrod's hand. "You did good deeds for these people today. With each healing you strengthened their faith and gave them hope. Those are the true gifts."

Sherrod said, "You are a good man, Charles." He winked and patted the man on his shoulder. "Now remember to watch it with the meat and eggs. And eat eight cherries a day."

Charles chuckled. "I'm doing good with it." He turned to walk away. "Y'all take care now."

Abby's puzzled expression brought a quick response from Sherrod. "Gout. Charles used to have awful spells with it."

"Cherries?"

Sherrod waved at a child who called goodbye to him. "Cherries relieve the pain and contain minerals like magnesium and potassium. But if he pays attention to his diet and avoids foods high in nucleic acid, he won't be as susceptible to it."

Abby was impressed. But she was slightly confused. "So, are you a healer or a root doctor?"

Sherrod appreciated her candor.

"I guess you could say I am a little of both." He stooped and pointed at a yellow dandelion flower on the ground at the edge of a clump of clover. "See this?"

Abby knelt down and looked at the beautiful flower growing close to the ground. "I see them everywhere," she answered as she touched the cool petals with her fingers.

Sherrod continued, "I can apply this single plant to arthritis, upset stomach, constipation, gout, boils and warts." He then pointed to a dogwood tree that stood at the edge of the forest like a leaning umbrella. "The dogwood bark reduces fever." Sherrod stood up. "I can make a gargle from the roots of a blackberry bush that will cure a sore throat and bleeding gums. Or, I can...." Sherrod looked at the people walking away across the meadow and then back at the forest behind him. He hesitated.

"Or, you can do what?" Abby knew his answer.

Sherrod seldom spoke of his gift. The proof of it was in his actions. But he wanted to answer Abby. He trusted her as he trusted his mother and Emily and Doc. He wanted her in that inner circle of people with whom he could speak freely. And yet, she was somehow different from them. Her very appearance in the meadow was like a meeting waiting to happen. A pre-ordained arrangement. The vision of a dream come true. Some would call it destiny.

Abby felt it, too. She wanted to be near Sherrod. It felt right. She wanted to hear his voice and ask him questions about his life. He intrigued her, awakening every desire and curiosity within her.

When the last of all who had come to the meadow that day had disappeared over the hill and there was only the two of them standing beside the oak tree, Sherrod answered Abby's question. "I am both. I treat them with the remedies of nature to show them the healing capacity of the natural world around them. The cures for most illnesses known to man are within reach in his own backyard. It is also within my power to touch and heal. That is born of a natural faith. I have it. But if the one who seeks my help does not have that faith, then I am rendered powerless."

Abby thought for a moment. "Then the faithless can call you a fraud?"

"Yes, they can. But seldom do the faithless come

to me. And when they do, I can see them for what they are before they open their mouths."

"The old, ragged man today?" Abby had wondered about that brief and uncomfortable encounter. "Is he an unbeliever?"

"He is a tempter. One who is sent to test me. To lure me away from my purpose."

"Do you know him?"

"I've seen him many times. But he never looks the same."

"And the man who challenged you. Nash Moseley." Abby cringed as she spoke his name. "What is he? Why did he come here?"

Sherrod searched pensively up the hill. "He is a clever one. He would not allow me to look directly into his eyes. That means there is something there that is not good at all. I think he has a connection to you. So be careful and avoid him. As far as his challenge to me, I sensed a darkness in him. A dark heart is what I suspect."

"A dark heart?" Abby's interest in Sherrod was growing every minute. She was beginning to understand why such mystery surrounded the man.

"Walk with me, and I will tell you about a dark heart." He led the young woman into the forest and walked beside her as he talked. "Just as there is goodness in the hearts of men, there is also evil. It is real. Not the imagined storybook kind of evil, but something darker and more sinister than one can comprehend. Evil is not found in nature. It is not in the wind of a hurricane or the fire of lightning. It is not in raging flood waters or a violent sea. These are natural occurrences to be aware of and avoided if possible. Evil is not found in a poisonous plant or an animal that stalks its prey. Remember that all things in nature have a purpose. True evil has its purpose, also. And that is to destroy the goodness of mankind from within. Evil's source is a patient and clever trickster. Its seeds of corruption are many, and it nurtures them well in those who are weak in faith and strong in will. No human being is unscathed by evil. It weaves in and out of our thoughts like a snake in the vine. It drops its seed in the curious and fertile minds of the doubters, then waits for it to take root into one's heart and soul. It wears a coat of innocence that hides the fangs of a serpent."

Sherrod stopped near a large granite boulder. He peeled a black and crusty flake of lichen from its surface and handed it to Abby. "Evil clouds a man's good intentions and darkens his heart and soul just as the lichen covers the grayness of the rock."

Abby held the lichen in her palm for a minute. She crunched it between her fingers. "So, who is worse?" she asked. "The tempter or the dark heart?"

Sherrod led her through a labyrinth of boulders as he answered. "Well, the tempter tries to lure you away from what is good by suggesting that you give in to desire and greed. If you do not give in, he will leave you for the next tempter's try. But the dark heart will not leave until he has ruined you. Even to the point of taking your life. They are put here and nurtured from birth to hunt those who walk in the light of the good spirit."

"So you are hunted by the tempters and the dark hearts?" Abby asked.

"All good people are hunted by them," Sherrod answered. "Especially me, and anyone who professes the word of the good spirit. If you walk in the light, you are a target."

"How many have come for you?" Abby could not imagine how Sherrod had lived his life. But she sensed that, although he was cautious, he was not afraid.

"More than I can say." He paused. "But they seldom come here, and never in the same place.

"I won't see the ragged man again. No one will know where he went after today. But if Nash Moseley is a dark heart, and I think he is, I will see him again. It is just a matter of time, now that he has found me and seen me at work."

Sherrod stopped walking and turned to Abby. "But there is something else about him that bothers me. And that is you. I saw the way he looked at you today, and I felt your fear toward him."

"He frightens me to death," Abby admitted.

"I think he found me through his pursuit of you, Abby."

Abby felt a tinge of guilt. "I'm sorry, Sherrod."

The young man shook his head. "Don't be. You did not knowingly bring him here. But I want you to watch out for him. Stay clear of him and alert the authorities if he continues to bother you."

"I will," Abby promised. "But what about you? Will he come back after you?"

Sherrod answered confidently. "The people of Buena

Vista will not listen to him if he tries to discredit me. But he has not finished his purpose. As I said before, it is just a matter of time. He cannot help it."

"How will you know?" Abby did not want anything to happen to Sherrod now that she had found him. Her passion was sudden and profound.

Sherrod smiled and looked around. "The trees will tell me. They are my friends."

"There's a lot about you I'd like to know, Sherrod Dane."

"We'll have plenty of time to talk, Abby. But right now I need to speak with Doc."

"He's gone to the tree you call Grandmother."

Sherrod pointed up the winding path. "My cabin is just around that turn. You can wait there while I go to see him."

Moments later, Abby rounded the bend in the path and followed Sherrod into the yard of the cabin nestled beneath the trees.

"This is my home," she heard him say.

But her attention was already drawn to words carved into the bark of a beech tree. Familiar words that recalled a little girl's hope.

Words. Meaningful and elusive. Phrases that linger in our minds. We hold dear to them and imagine the voices that uttered them, whether from a child, friend, or lover.

A wife speaks the words "I love you" to her son, her husband, and her parents, gathered near her, and the meaning is obvious to all who hear it.

On a warm June night in 1938, Laura Dane stood at the bedside of her son and wept silently. She had done everything she could to see that he would be taken care of. Words had been spoken. Promises made. She bent over and kissed the boy on his forehead and touched his soft, blonde hair. "I will love you, always," she whispered. Moonglow illuminated the boy's face as his mother stood there. *So much like his father*, she thought. Especially his eyes. Hazel-blue. She wanted to see them again, but she did not awaken him. Instead, she turned and walked out of the room. She held to the bannister as she walked downstairs. Tears formed on her cheeks. The moon brought light to the interior of the cabin. She touched a photograph at the end of the fireplace mantle. It was of the two of them sitting on a rock in the meadow. Then she opened the front door and felt a warm breeze on her face. She leaned against the door frame and took a breath of air. The sweet fragrance of meadow flowers drifted through the woods. So weak, she stepped onto the porch and carefully walked down the steps. The cool, smooth bark of the beech tree felt good on her cheek as she leaned her frail body against it. She longed for the one she loved. To hear his voice once more. To feel the warmth of his arms around her. But she knew she could not wait. This was her time. Her heart pounded as she reached into her pocket and retrieved the penknife he had given their son. Tears blurred her vision as she carved for him her last words. Words she had whispered to Sherrod held a different meaning for the man who rushed to her side from out of the darkness and caught her in his arms as she collapsed at the base of the tree.

A smile formed on the lips of Laura Dane as she touched his face for the last time and died in his caress.

The man who loved her held her close to his heart and whispered her name over and over. His tears glistened in the moonlight and fell upon her still lips.

The moon is a silent witness. A quiet keeper of secrets. But on the night that Laura Dane died, the moon was not the only witness. For, on that night, a boy stood in the doorway of the cabin. He watched and listened and wept softly, unseen by the man who had loved his mother.

Nash Moseley sat behind the wheel of his car and pounded on the dashboard with his fist. He threw his head back and wiped his face with his hands. "I get it now," he said aloud while lighting a cigarette.

A group of people walked on the side of the road toward cars parked in front of him. He saw their approach in his rearview mirror and rolled down his window. He extended his arm out and flicked the ash off the end of his cigarette with his middle finger. "He's a root doctor, you know," he spoke loudly as the people walked by his car. "Nothin' but a tree-huggin', backwoods root doctor. Got you all believin' he can walk on water."

The group of people did not pause or comment. They did not look at Nash or acknowledge he was even there. That angered him more. "I've seen his kind at cheap fairs ever since I can remember."

The people opened their car doors and started their engines and pulled away.

Nash reached under his car seat and felt for a bottle he knew was there. When he found it, he brought it up, unscrewed the top, and swallowed its remaining contents in two gulps. The whiskey caused his eyes to water. He wanted more, but it was Sunday and the liquor stores were closed. He screwed the top back on and started to toss the empty bottle into the woods on the opposite side of the road when he heard a man's voice.

"Taking a little shot or two of courage, are you?" Charles Pauley was not smiling. He had seen and heard Nash's behavior in the meadow, and he was not one to let such things pass. Charles had been a deputy sheriff for years in Amherst County before he retired and moved to Buena Vista. His years as an officer of the law had left him a pretty good judge of character. He seldom missed on his first impressions of folks. Intuitively, he knew that Nash was a bad apple. There was no provocation for the scene he had caused in the meadow that day. Just a troubled soul looking for a fix. Charles knew his kind. He had heard talk of Nash Moseley around town. Co-workers at the bottle company did not like him. Especially the women. The men laughed him off and generally ignored him.

Then there was the Borden girl. Susie was the oldest daughter of Jim and Ellen Borden, a well-thought-of couple who struggled to give their three daughters all they could. Susie, a pretty blonde who should have known better, became involved with Nash and ended up being sent away to live with relatives in Maryland, instead of entering her junior year at Hollins College, where she had been a stand-out student. Her parents were crushed. The whole town was talking about it for a while. There was a rumor that Susie had come away with a black eye when she confronted Nash about doing the right thing. Threats were made. The law was called in. And then, it all quieted down.

Charles Pauley liked the Bordens. He was fond of the Borden girls and did not like what had happened to Susie in the least.

"What's it to you?" Nash sneered up at the older man.

Charles did not back down at all. He stood with an air of authority, his short, strong arms folded across his chest and his legs apart. "Well, Moseley, you're not much to me at all," he began. "But Sherrod Dane is. He and his family are well thought of around here, and what happened in the meadow today was uncalled for."

"Yeah, right." Nash rolled his eyes. "I'm really broken up about it."

Charles felt the blood rushing through his veins.

His heartbeat quickened with his anger. But he tried his best to mask it. "Look," he said. "Some of those men up there today were about to take care of you, had it not been for Sherrod stopping them."

Nash faked a shudder. "Well then, I must thank Sherrod All Mighty for stepping in and saving me."

Charles shook his head in resignation. "You are a bad one. But you really need to back off," he warned. "You just don't know Sherrod Dane."

Nash inhaled the smoke from his cigarette and blew it out in a long, thin stream toward the man who was offering him advice.

"Thanks for the warning, Pops." He started his car. "I'll treasure our little conversation."

Charles watched Nash pull away. He mashed the cigarette Nash had dropped out the window before he left. There was a feeling of dread inside him. It was gut level. An intuitive anticipation. He shook his head as he walked to his truck. He knew that Nash Moseley was bad. But even with all his years in law enforcement, he could not have imagined the evil that dwelt in Nash's soul.

Doctor Frank Tynes had not stepped a foot in the woods on Elephant Mountain in over a year. That was when he had last spoken with Sherrod. It had not gone well. He had demanded too much. He had expected that Sherrod would do something that was against the rules. Just that one time. Doc should have known better. He knew the rules. Sherrod had told him how it worked. Break the rules, step over the boundaries and the power is lost. Do not give into the tempters, or the foundation of one's faith would begin to erode. "A faithless healer does not exist," Sherrod had told him.

Doc had tempted Sherrod. He knew it in his heart, and it bludgeoned his thoughts each day. But what else could he have done? Science and medicine could not save Emily from the cancer that had entered her body—the awful demon that sapped her strength and forced his own guilt.

In fear and helplessness he had asked Sherrod to stop it. To rid her body of the vile thing that would take her away and leave him alone.

Doc could see in his mind the tears in Sherrod's eyes when he said in a sad and disappointed voice, "This will bring about her passing. I have looked into her soul. I cannot stop what is meant to be."

"But it is Emily, my wife. The woman who loves you and raised you as her own child." Doc had pleaded selfishly. "Sherrod, I have seen you perform miracles with the touch of your hand. The source of your power must recognize the goodness of the woman. I beg you to heal her. Do what I can't do."

Sherrod had known Doc's feeling of helplessness. He had felt the man's fear of impending loss when he was a young child. But he could not give in, not even to his heart's inclination to save his adopted mother. "Her spirit is being called to fulfill its destiny," Sherrod had explained. "I cannot interfere with the spirit's journey."

Sherrod's refusal was the end of Doc's hope. In desperate anger, he had lashed out. "Then perhaps you are just a root doctor," he said accusingly. "Nothing more than a medicine man and mountain trickster whose luck has not yet run its course." He had not believed one word of his accusation and had carried the shame of it ever since.

Doc stayed deep in the woods as he walked around the meadow toward the cabin, avoiding the gathering. It was his way of separating science and religion. But as the years had passed, he found himself wondering if a blending of the two would not bring about the best for all. He had lived long enough to know that faith did not bow to the limitations of science. He performed his miracles with common-sense advice and tested medicine. But Sherrod performed his through his knowledge of nature and his faith in a power granted to him. That kind of faith transcends understanding.

A familiar trail wound through the maze of granite stones, oaks, and hemlock trees. It was a trail Doc knew well. He paused at the beech tree in the yard for a minute and traced with his fingers the words carved into its bark. He walked up on the porch and opened the front door. Everything was the same as it had always been. He stepped over to the hearth and looked at a framed picture of Sherrod and his mother sitting together on a rock in the meadow. Their smiles were identical. The black and white photograph captured the characteristics of their faces, but could not touch the brilliance of the moment it was taken. Doc studied the other photographs along the mantle before he turned and walked out the door, closing it behind him. He stood on the porch and looked at his pocket watch. The shadow of a bird flying over the treetops brought his attention up to a green forest canopy through which he saw a blue, cloudless sky. He left the porch and walked around to the back of the cabin, where he struck an unmarked path into the woods.

The grandmother tree was at the crown of a hollow between two steep ridges a quarter of a mile away. It was a good place to meet Sherrod.

"Did you carve this?" Abby traced the letters in the bark of the tree with her fingers.

Sherrod smiled and shook his head. "No. My mother did." He watched Abby's delicate fingers as she finished her tracing. "Your birth mother?" Abby asked.

"Yes."

"What was her name?" Abby turned and leaned her back against the tree. Her eyes were not afraid to search Sherrod's as she spoke.

"Laura." Sherrod was aware that Abby was allowing him to see into her eyes. He could not hold back his smile.

"Tell me about her." Abby pushed away from the tree and walked over to the porch.

Sherrod followed her up the steps and opened the front door. "She was a beautiful woman." He ushered her in as he talked.

Abby felt at home immediately. She walked over to the stone hearth and looked at the photographs as she listened.

Sherrod closed the front door and continued. "She loved to read and write poetry. Mostly nature-related works. She was funny and laughed a lot. She was talented, too."

"Oh?" Abby saw the same smile on the faces of mother and son in a photograph.

"Yes." Sherrod walked over to a corner of the room and picked up a guitar. "She played this."

Abby saw the instrument and put her hands over her chest in surprise. "A Martin," she said in awe. "Where did she get this?"

Sherrod could see Abby's enthusiasm and handed the guitar over to her. "Do you play?"

Abby took the guitar and sat down on the sofa. She strummed it and brought it into tune. The strings were old but still sounded better than the Black Diamond strings she had played on her old guitar for so long. She played a few chords and marveled at the rich tone. "I've played since I was a little girl," she said while re-tuning the strings. When she was done, she plucked out a sweet, short melody.

Sherrod was impressed. "My mother could play anything she heard on the radio. She made up songs, too."

Abby smiled and played a jazzy up-tempo number

Sherrod had never heard. He clapped his hands when it was over. "That's really great."

Abby laughed and handed back the guitar. "It's really a good one," she said, looking around the room. "How long has she been gone?"

"Twenty years. I was eight." Sherrod turned his head to the side and scratched his eyebrow with his thumb.

"What about your father?" Abby wanted to know everything.

"I get to ask you some questions, don't I?" Sherrod stood up and walked toward the front door.

"You're going to leave me here." Abby stood up.

"Doc and I will be back soon." He opened the door. "He's waiting for me." He stepped out onto the porch, then poked his head back in. "Make yourself at home. We'll be back within the hour." An old Herschedes mantle clock began chiming the hour as he winked and closed the door behind him. It was six o'clock.

Abby stood there for the duration of the clock's chiming and then began exploring the spacious cabin.

By the time Sherrod arrived at the grandmother tree, Doc had already been there for a couple of hours. "Am I late?" he asked.

Doc had watched Sherrod's approach through the

forest which was dappled in evening sunlight. He was impressed with how the young man moved. Graceful yet responsive to his surroundings.

Doc arose from his cool, mossy seat at the base of the maple tree and smiled. "You told me when you were a boy that the clock of nature chimes twice. Once at daybreak, and once at sunset. Every minute in between is...."

Sherrod put out his hand and finished Doc's sentence. "An opportunity to find one's place in the world." He grinned. "And what about the night, Doc? Do you remember?"

"Of course I do," the man replied. "Time waits while the body rests, and the soul seeks reconciliation with the good spirit in the light of the moon and stars."

Sherrod nodded his head and smiled.

Doc shook Sherrod's hand. "Today my place is here at the tree you call Grandmother." Doc sat back down.

Sherrod sat in the leaves opposite him. "I'm glad you came. It's been a long time."

"That's my fault, Sherrod." Doc felt emotional and looked off into the shadows for a moment before he looked back at Sherrod's face and continued. "You know I didn't mean the things I said." He looked down at the ground and picked up a dried maple leaf. He twirled its curled stem between his forefinger and thumb. "It's just that I couldn't fathom the thought of losing her." Tears came to his eyes, with a whisper on his lips, "Not my Emily."

Sherrod looked at the face of the man who had

raised him. Frank Tynes was such a part of his life that he could not recall a time when he was not there for him. The past year had been hard on them both. They were unaccustomed to periods of silence between them, until that day when harsh words had been spoken. Before that, Sherrod had always been able to talk and share his life with Doc. He had missed their walks in the woods and their long conversations beside trout streams and crackling campfires. He had missed Doc and Emily's voices and laughter, their picnics in the meadow, and his visits to the home where they brought him after his mother had died. He wanted his family back. But he had waited for Doc to settle his anger and fear.

Sherrod had prayed for this day. In his heart he knew it would come. But he could not force it. Not with Doc, and not with himself. Sherrod had to believe that the good spirit would urge the acceptance of Emily's illness in the hearts of those who loved her most and would miss her unmeasurably. "I come to her at night, Doc," Sherrod confessed. "She tells me that you are quiet and distant in the house. She worries about you. She misses you, and you are right there with her."

Doc sighed and dropped the maple leaf. "For a long time I think that instinctively I have tried to distance myself from the fear of losing her. But in the process, I have brought about an even worse separation. She must feel so alone. It's just hard to face the reality of it each and every day. So I continue the house calls and the office visits. And then when I can and should be with her, I go to my study and stare at meaningless pages in medical journals. Abby, the girl I brought here today, the one who helps me in my practice, speaks more to Emily now than I do."

Sherrod had seen something in Abby's eyes that made him aware of her interest in him. He wondered about her. What had she learned about his family? What had Emily told her? It had seemed strange to him that although he was the one who could see into the souls of people, she had somehow looked into his. Hers was the face he had seen in a dream. She puzzled him and fascinated him at once. He had not yet looked long into her eyes. But he had looked long enough to know that he wanted to see more. "It has been good that Em has had Abby to talk to these months," he heard himself say. "But she needs you. You know that, Doc. This is the time to say the things you must. This is the time to be close to her and cherish every minute you have with her."

Doc swallowed hard and wiped his palms on his knees. He stood up and looked down at Sherrod. "I know that everything you say is true. And I am going to try." He looked away. "But I'm afraid."

Sherrod stood up. "Afraid of what? You've been married to the woman for over forty years." Sherrod stepped in front of Doc and tried to look into his eyes.

Doc looked down. "Don't, Sherrod. Don't do that." He turned and placed his hands on the maple tree. "I wish I could hear the things, feel the things you do out here. I wish I could touch the trees and know the answers to life's problems. But I can't. I'm just a man. A man with flaws I've kept to myself. You don't want to know what's in my soul, Sherrod." A tear left the corner of Doc's eye as he spoke. "But you must know that I am sorry for what I said to you. And that I will try to tell Emily the things that are in my heart." He dropped his hands to his side.

Sherrod touched Doc's shoulder. "Harsh words cannot break our bond. Em needs you more than anything now. Go to her. Be there for her, just as she has been there for you."

"There's not much time, is there? I know it. She's so weak."

Sherrod looked at the growing shadows in the woods. He looked back at Doc. His compassion for the man was strong. "There is still time," he advised. "Say those things you need to say. Your heart and soul are ready."

Doc knew Sherrod was right. "What does Grandmother have to say about all this?" he asked while admiring the girth of the maple tree.

Sherrod put his hand on the tree and closed his eyes for a moment. "She says the truth will make you strong." He opened his eyes and smiled. "It's that simple. Face the truth."

Abby slowly walked through each room in the cabin, taking it all in. Every photograph on the fireplace mantle and on the walls shed light on the mystery of the man who lived there. Each step she took brought her closer to him in ways she could not fully understand.

The cabin was quiet, but in its silence she perceived a history she could not have known. She could almost hear a child's voice and laughter. She imagined the boy and his mother sitting together on the couch in front of the fireplace on wintry nights. Books were read aloud and stories were told. Abby paused at a picture, framed and placed on the wall where she turned to go upstairs. In the picture, Laura Dane stood smiling next to the beech tree in the front yard. Her long, blonde hair glowed in a dazzle of sunlight. Her smile was fetching, the look in her eyes alluring. Abby wondered who had taken the photograph. The angle of the shot suggested it was not a child. She was sure that the person behind the lens of the camera had drawn something from the soul of Laura Dane that was meant for no other.

Sherrod's bedroom was sparsely furnished with hand-made pieces. A rocking chair sat in the corner of the room. Next to it, a table and lamp. The bed, a walnut sleigh-type, had leaves and acorns intricately carved into it. It was positioned next to the double window of the room. A thin, patched quilt of earthy colors and two over-stuffed pillows made the bed seem warm and inviting. The bed's headboard was reflected in the mirror that sat atop a walnut chest-of-drawers. A tall, matching wardrobe balanced the furnishings in the room.

Abby walked down the hallway and stepped into a study. Its walls were aligned with shelves of books. Wood carvings and black and white photographs were interspersed among the volumes. A large oak desk stacked with hand-written papers dominated the center of the room. Although she was intrigued, Abby turned her attention to a photograph of Doc and Sherrod displayed in a frame next to a pen set. She had seen the photograph before, but not with such clarity. Now she picked it up, walked over to the window, and explored the images. She touched the glass over the faces in the picture and then suddenly gasped and put her fingers to her open lips. In that moment, she realized the one thing that no one had voiced.

Abby set the photograph back in its place. She turned and leaned against the window. The blue haze was reaching up and out of the folds of the mountains, reclaiming the slopes and ridges and hiding their secrets. Abby thought back over her time spent in Buena Vista. She remembered her conversations with Emily and Doc. She had felt the tension between them, the guarded silence when Sherrod's name was spoken. She had seen the protective wall from those who knew him.

At first Abby had not understood at all. Then she had begun to think that people wanted to protect Sherrod from the outside world. That alone made sense. For it was a world that would invade him and ruin his ability to do his work as it was intended to be done — quietly and out of the spy glasses of the media. The tempters and the dark hearts were bad enough. Reporters would have driven him away. The people of Buena Vista did not want that. But there was something else that, if known, had never been spoken. A truth untold for the best reasons.

At the moment of her revelation, Abby's heart grew for the people in that mountain community. Now she was one of them. She had had an inner drive to know Sherrod Dane since the day she came into contact with his family. Before that, he was a nameless man she knew she would someday meet. That was written on her heart the night she watched her parents dance in the moonglow and heard the promises they made to one another. Abby knew that she had found Sherrod because it was meant to be that way. Now she wondered how he felt about her. Had he also been aware of an attraction beyond explanation? Certainly, Sherrod would have recognized it and understood it even more than she. Time would tell. Abby knew it would. She had that kind of faith.

Abby would not talk of her discovery. She would join in silence with those who knew the secret that could never be spoken. But she did wonder about those closest to it. She could not help but be concerned for them because she had come to love them.

Abby walked out of the study and down the stairs. When she opened the front door, Doc and Sherrod were coming around the corner of the cabin.

"Well, hello, Abby." Doc smiled and approached her.

Abby walked to the edge of the porch. She put her

hands on her hips. "I was beginning to worry about the two of you, traipsing around in the hills so late in the day," she scolded teasingly. "I was just about to come out looking for you."

Doc chuckled and looked around at Sherrod. "She's gotten right protective of me, Sherrod. Sounds a little like Emily, doesn't she?"

Sherrod walked up beside Doc and put his hands in his pockets. He looked at Abby, and for an instant he was speechless. All he could think of was how beautiful she was, standing there on his front porch. And how natural it all seemed. "I'm glad you waited, Abby," he finally managed to say. "After all you have seen today, I would not have blamed you if you had walked back on your own." He smiled, then added, "But I'm really happy you stayed."

Doc walked up on the porch and sat down in one of the high-back rocking chairs. He removed his hat and motioned for Abby to sit down in the other rocker. "Sherrod and I were talking on the way in about an idea I've had lately." He waited for Abby to sit down. Sherrod joined them on the porch and sat on the floor, his back against a post.

"What is it, Doc?" Abby asked.

Doc looked at Sherrod, then back at Abby. "Well, when Woodrow and Lucy Marsden passed away a few years back, I bought their place. Their children live away from here and didn't want it and, well, I just thought it would be a good investment."

"Woodrow and Lucy were really good neighbors," Sherrod spoke up. "Our's were the only homes on the mountain. We looked out for each other for a long time."

Abby knew of the Marsdens. She remembered that Emily had said Woodrow and Lucy were at the Dane cabin the night Sherrod was born. "Emily told me you were close to them, Sherrod." Abby rocked her chair a little.

Sherrod smiled and nodded his head. He could not take his eyes off her as Doc continued.

"They were good people, for sure. But back to my idea. I don't want to rent the house or sell it. Sherrod keeps an eye on the place and his truck in the garage."

"There is no road up here," Sherrod interjected.

Doc shook his head. "No, there's no road past that rutty mule trail we call Indian Gap trace. But it's good enough for Abby to drive in to the Marsden's place and call it home, if she wants it." Doc waited for his words to take effect.

Abby had seen the Marsden place only once, when she and Doc had stopped there to check on things while they were en route to a patient's house. She had walked around the house with him but had not gone in. It was a tidy, wood-frame home, old, but in good condition. Very secluded. The house was nestled in a grove of big oak trees. There was a double garage next to the house and a barn and other outbuildings behind it. Doc had told her one hundred acres went with it. Some grown-over fields, an apple orchard, and lots of big woods.

"What is the rent, Doc?" Abby stopped rocking and turned in her chair.

Doc laughed and looked at Sherrod. Then he looked back at Abby. "Here's the deal, young lady." He smiled. "You live there and take care of the house, write your book, and work for me, and there's no rent. It's as simple as that. For as long as you want it."

Abby was taken aback. "But why, Doc?" she asked. "I mean, that would be great, but what about Emily? I'm there for...."

Doc interrupted. "I know you are there for her, Abby. But so am I. Or I will be. During the days, she'll still have you and me and Jesse Lou and Henri. And at night, she'll have me. And that's as it should be." Doc waited for his words to sink in. Then he continued. "Besides, you are never going to finish writing that book of yours if I don't give you some free time. And I want to read your book someday. Now, what do you say?"

Abby looked over at Sherrod. He raised his eyebrows and cupped his ear with his hand as if waiting to hear her answer.

"You're not trying to get rid of me are you?"

Doc pushed back in his chair. "No way, Abby. I'm trying to keep you."

Abby was choked with emotion when she spoke. "You know I love you and Emily. I love this town and want to stay. I want to write my book and...." She could not finish her thoughts.

Doc stood up and Abby rose from her chair and stepped into his open arms. He patted her on the back reassuringly. "I know," he said, offering her his handkerchief. "You're going to do a lot of things in your lifetime. But right now, you need a place of your own. A quiet place to write that book. How about it?"

Abby touched the corner of her eyes with the handkerchief. "I'd love to live there, if it's okay with Emily and…." She glanced at Sherrod, but did not speak his name.

Doc opened his pocket watch and looked at the time. "I'll talk to Emily about it, and Sherrod can show you the house tonight then bring you home." He tapped the glass on his watch face with his finger. "I've got to go. Jesse Lou's got supper ready, and Emily will be worried." He started down the porch steps. "I'll get Jesse Lou to set aside a plate for you."

"She can have supper with me, Doc," Sherrod called out as Doc hurried down the pathway.

"Will you?" Sherrod asked Abby quietly.

She agreed with a nod.

Doc waved his hand without looking back. "I'll leave the porch light on for you, Abby," he called out just before he disappeared behind a rock at the edge of the yard.

Abby's heart beat fast as she turned toward Sherrod. She did not know what to say. Her day had just been too eventful. "It'll be dark by the time he gets to the meadow. Can he find his way?" she asked.

"He will be fine. Doc taught me how to walk in the woods at night."

"I don't want to impose on you."

"Don't be silly." Sherrod opened the door to the cabin and waited while Abby walked in. "I've got fresh trout in the fridge, and there is no telling what is in that basket that Charles brought to the meadow today. I'm sure it's way more than I can eat alone." Sherrod followed Abby into the cabin and closed the door behind them. He was unaware of the small breeze that kicked into the leaves of the trees and caused a light rustle over the entire mountain. But Sherrod would have known its meaning. He knew the silent language and how the wind gave voice to it.

By the time Sherrod and Abby finished supper, it was after nine o'clock. Abby insisted on cleaning up afterwards, and Sherrod did not resist. He washed and she dried.

"How did a girl from Newport News learn to fry trout like that?" Sherrod asked while putting away the last plate.

Abby laughed. She walked into the den and sat down on the couch. "When I was a little girl, I watched my grandmother fry up ocean trout and flounder that my dad would bring home from the seafood stand just down the block from where we lived. She would let me help her butter them up and roll them in corn meal. Fish are fish. You fry one, you've fried them all. It just doesn't take as long to get those little native trout of yours on a plate."

Sherrod sat down at the end of the couch. He turned to face Abby. "Have you ever gone fishing?"

"My dad took me out to some farm ponds in the country a few times. I was pretty good at it, too."

"Would you like to go with me sometime?" Sherrod asked hopefully.

Abby did not have to ponder her answer. "I'd love

to." Even she thought she sounded eager. "Where do you fish for trout around here?"

"Well, there are streams all through the mountain range. I like the Pedlar and the Piney Rivers. You will be surprised at the size of the streams they are in." Sherrod got up and lifted a framed picture from a corner cabinet. "This is my mother standing beside a little creek just two ridges over from us." He handed Abby the picture and sat back down.

Abby noticed a little blonde-haired boy in the background. She turned the picture around and extended it toward Sherrod. "That's you reaching your hand into that pool behind her, isn't it?"

Sherrod looked at the picture. "Yes."

Abby looked at the picture again. "Who took this photograph?"

Sherrod reached over and Abby handed the photograph back to him. He stood up and walked over to the corner cabinet, where he replaced the silver-framed photograph. "Doc took it." Sherrod walked to the front door and looked out. The mantle clock chimed the half hour. "We had better get on down to the Marsden's place." He opened the door. "It's gotten a little cooler. Do you want a jacket?"

Abby stood up and walked toward the open door. She could feel the night air on her bare arms. "Do you mind?"

"Not at all." Sherrod pulled a light-weight jacket from a rack beside the door and held it while Abby slipped her arms into it. Then he walked over to a table drawer and brought out a small hand-held flashlight. "This is for you," he said handing it to Abby.

"Where's yours?" she asked.

"I know that trail with my eyes closed. You follow me and watch out for rocks and tree roots along the way."

The walk through the night forest was a first for Abby. The sounds she had heard from front porches or sidewalks during an evening walk were all around her. There was a sky with bright stars, but the trees' canopy shut her off from that world of light. She had never known such utter darkness, and she was apprehensive about it.

One who lives close to nature is sensitive to all living things. The wind and water speak a language others have forgotten through the evolution that has separated them from their true origin. They have lost the ability to understand the songs of the birds or the calls of the animals. Or to even care. Plants and the trees, the oldest of living things, have become invisible to them.

Sherrod Dane's connection to the natural world was a great part of his gift. He could feel when Abby became fearful of her surroundings. That is when he stopped and turned to her. "Stand close to me and turn off your light. Don't be afraid. Just listen."

Abby stepped forward without speaking. She switched off the flashlight and put it in her jacket pocket. The blackness was vast and alive. The night creatures voiced their presence in waves of sound. A bobcat screamed in the distance, and Abby reached out her hands. Instinctively, Sherrod embraced her.

He felt her cheek on his chest and the beating of her heart as he pulled her closer to him. "Don't be afraid," he repeated softly as he held her in his arms. "A star-filled sky is just above the trees. And there is nothing here that will harm you. Believe me, Abby. Just breathe and accept the voices of nature."

Sherrod's gentle words calmed Abby. Strength and fearlessness were in his words and the tone of his voice. Nothing bad could happen to her in his presence. She felt that, and it gave her courage. She did not want him to let go.

For a full minute they stood there without moving until finally Abby said, "I guess I'd better turn the flashlight back on."

Sherrod thought her voice blended well with the breeze that rustled the treetops. He squeezed her delicate shoulders and said, "Soon we will be in the meadow, and you will see a spectacular sky." He turned and led the way.

Several minutes later, the man and woman walked into the meadow. The vibrant colors of a summer day had bowed to the heavenly brilliance of the moon and stars.

Abby stood close beside Sherrod and watched in silent awe as a falling star arched across the sky. She felt the warmth of Sherrod's hand as he reached over and cupped her cool fingers in his. She looked at his face and listened as he spoke softly and elegantly:

Now swims the moon along the Milky Way
In burnished splendor; and the hours of night

March forth like conquerors who hold mild sway,
Dispensing golden dreams, and rest, and light,
Alike on cottage, hut, or princely hall,
A peaceful unison, dowered alike on all.

When he finished his recitation, Sherrod turned and looked upon the face of the woman whose hands he now raised to his heart. She was meant for him, of that there was no doubt. Stars sparkled in the pools of her eyes as nature cast its spell and their lips touched. A star fell across the sky, but neither one witnessed it. With eyes closed, they were lost in the blissful moment of their hearts' realizations. Drawn like the tides, they submitted to the power that had guided their spirits toward one another. There was no consciousness of fear. No questioning of their hearts. Only an unexplained fulfillment of what was meant to be. Whispered words on moistened lips heightened their desire as they lay down upon a bed of clover and became as nature had intended them to be. One in spirit and body.

Later that night, Abby lay in Sherrod's arms. The cool breeze dried the sweat of her body as she turned on her side and touched his lips with her fingers. "Did you know I was coming?" she asked softly.

Sherrod turned his head toward her. He kissed her fingers. "I have somehow known since the night I saw your face as a child in my dream. A face in moonglow."

Abby placed her hand on Sherrod's chest. She could feel his heart beating. "When I was a little girl

I used to wish upon the moon that someday I would find you. A man that I could love the way my mother loved my father. I prayed every night. And when the moon was full, I would pray in its light. I thought that if I knelt there at my window in the moonlight, God could see me and would listen." Abby leaned toward Sherrod and laid her cheek against his chest. "When I lost my family, I stopped praying." She bit her lip and wiped away a tear. And then in a soft and broken voice she said, "But I never stopped believing that you were there."

Sherrod heard the emotion in Abby's voice. It touched his heart. He knew that kind of loneliness. He knew about wishes and prayers, and about waiting for answers and watching for signs.

Sherrod kissed Abby on the forehead and took in the fragrance of her hair. Gently he urged her over on her back, his forearm her pillow. He had memorized the features of her face in the first moments of their meeting that afternoon. He had looked into her eyes long enough to know she was the one. Yes, he had known she was coming. But he had not known just how beautiful she would be or that her voice would awaken his heart like a spring morning. Even her whisper captivated him. "We wished and prayed under the light of the same moon, Abby. And the good spirit heard us."

There was so much Abby wanted to say, but the words fell away until only a few mattered. She smiled through tears of joy and spoke. "I love you, Sherrod Dane. With my heart and soul, I do."

A tear coursed down Sherrod's cheek and fell upon

her breast. He touched her face with his hand. "If you wish, I will marry you in a church down in the village. But tonight, I give you my heart here in the meadow, with the moon and the stars and the good spirit our only witnesses." He lowered his head and kissed Abby tenderly on the lips. "Whisper those words again to me, Abby, so that I might take them into my lungs and embrace them with my soul."

Their lips barely touched as Abby again whispered the commitment of her heart.

Sherrod breathed in her words, and Abby felt the strength and the nature of the man she was destined to love. Time stood still as their joy came in waves until, finally, they lay still in each other's arms. Abby listened to his heartbeat, and Sherrod heard the silent language that surrounded them.

Frank Tynes closed the door behind him as he left the office of Reverend Roy Thomas. The sun was shining as he walked along the sidewalk toward his house at the corner of Chestnut Avenue and 21st Street. The Buena Vista Baptist Church was forty yards behind him when he stopped and found the gap between trees where he could see Elephant Mountain and the granite outcrop that looked like a rock wall on the face of the mountain's western side. It was here on the sidewalk or out in the road where people would sometimes wait for Sherrod to make an appearance on the crest of the outcrop. Word of a sighting would send the townspeople in need of his help up to the meadow. Sherrod would normally make his appearance on the mountain on a Sunday afternoon if he was home. It was uncanny how many times Doc had heard from someone who needed Sherrod's help and had met with him although their visit to the meadow was unannounced. Sherrod had once told Doc that it was the trees that told him when he was needed. Doc had read in a science magazine that studies were being made into the possibility that there was some form of communication among all plant life. There had been nothing substantiated. No one was offering college courses yet at Southern Seminary or anywhere else on tree language. But trees, more than any other living thing, somehow summoned the spirit of men to seek their beauty and wisdom. Since the arrival of the Europeans in North America, the ripe, old hardwood forests and oceans of evergreens had fallen in the course of progress. Men tore them down as if they were an endless resource. And yet, there were those who recognized not only the beauty but also the importance of the oldest living things on earth.

Doc recalled the day when a young Sherrod had tearfully begged him not to cut down the old walnut tree that grew at the back of the house on Chestnut Avenue and stretched its limbs out over the porch roof. "Don't be like those who are heartless toward nature," the boy had said. "This is a living thing that is wise and beautiful." Sherrod had stood close to the tree while he defended it. He had even called it by name. "Jonathan." Emily had sided with the boy and in the end, Doc gave in and, instead, had the walnut tree limbed. It had grown back over the years and now swept the roof with its branches. No one, aside from Sherrod and Emily, understood why he allowed it to stay. *If man cannot re-learn to live in harmony with the nature around him and continues his greedy destruction of the earth's garden, then someday his children will choke and die at the expense of his failure.* Sherrod had written that in a school essay when he was a teenager. It was not a line one could forget.

Three weeks had passed since their meeting at the grandmother tree. In that time Doc had not gone more than a day or two without seeing Sherrod and talking with him. The visits were good and always at night. Sometimes Sherrod would walk in and find Doc in his study or sitting with Emily. And sometimes Doc would hear voices and find him sitting in the window seat upstairs talking with her. Sherrod could make her laugh, where she only smiled for Doc. Whenever Doc detected the fragrance of meadow flowers in the house, he knew Sherrod had been there. He was aware of their special bond.

The sun on Doc's face felt good. He closed his eyes for a minute, then opened them and blinked. He looked up at the mountain again. There was no white shirt. He smiled to himself and walked along the sidewalk toward his house. Perhaps Sherrod was with Abby, teaching her the trees. Calling them by name. Explaining to her the things he could not share with others. Abby was good for him. Emily had said that they were in love after Sherrod brought Abby to dinner last week. Doc agreed. It was evident. He and Emily felt as if it must have happened when the two met in the meadow. Abby had not returned home until well after midnight that night. She evidently had not seen the Marsden's place that night. The next day she drove up to meet Sherrod for the house tour. Three days later, she moved into the house along Indian Gap Run. She still came to the Tynes' home early on Monday through Friday and left by three o'clock in the afternoon. The weekdays were the same as they had been since Abby had come to town, but the evenings had changed. Now Doc spent as much time as he could with his wife. Henri and Jesse Lou usually left after supper, and the house became quiet except for the soft conversations of the two people who had lived there together for so many years. They played gin rummy, scrabble, and chess. And they both agreed they had no need for television at all. Radio in the morning and an evening newspaper were quite sufficient to keep them abreast of the news. At seven o'clock Doc had his brandy and Emily her glass of wine. They did not entertain, so visits from Sherrod and Abby on the past two Saturdays were welcomed and enjoyed. Doc liked to hear Emily laugh, and it was good to have young people in the house.

Doc crossed 21st Street and walked to the side door of the house. Jesse Lou met him at the door. The big woman wore a worried expression on her face. "Miz Emily says she ain't wantin' to eat no supper, Doc Tynes." Jesse Lou walked back into the kitchen while she talked. "I tells her she need to be eatin' somethin', but she gots her mind set on not doin' it."

Doc closed the door and followed Jesse Lou in. He did not speak.

Henri came into the kitchen and set a bowl of soup, a roll and a salad on a tray. She poured iced tea into a tall, thin glass and placed it on the tray. "Yo' steak and tato' is already in the den, Doc Tynes," Henri spoke quietly as she opened a drawer and brought out silverware and placed it on a cloth napkin beside the soup bowl on the tray. "There now," she said. "Miz Emily say she ain't gonna eat." Henri put her hands on her hips. "What you wants me to do, Doc Tynes?"

Doc pulled out his pocket watch and looked at the time. "Henri, you and Jesse Lou go on home to your families now," he said. "I'll take the tray."

"You sho' you don't wants me to stay an' clean up, Doc Tynes? 'Cause I will, an' I don't mind at all." Henri's offer was sincere.

"No. That's all right, Henri," Doc replied.

"If'n you needs us, jest call." Jesse Lou wrapped a thin shawl around her shoulders and walked to the back door.

Henri followed reluctantly. "We be seein' you on Monday then."

"Have a good weekend, ladies." Doc heard the back door close before he finished his sentence. He picked up the food tray and carefully walked out of the kitchen.

Abby sat alone on the side porch of Sherrod's cabin, absorbed in the silence of the mountains. A pale vapor lifted from the folds of the hills as a blue veil settled over the mountain sides, cushioned in evergreens and summer foliage. Ripples from the stream that flowed in the hollow far below the cabin were like golden sparkles through the tree branches. Abby leaned back and hugged her knees. She looked up at a cloudless sky and knew that soon it would be crowded with stars. It was all beautiful in her eyes. She thought how strange it was that she had never noticed it with such clarity. She had looked at the mountains and the stars in the sky before. She was aware of the trees and flowers and plants. But until now, she had never really appreciated their beauty and importance. And it had never occurred to her to listen to them. The wind was just the wind, and the rain made plants grow. She had never connected the things of nature with a language. There was so much she wanted to know. So much to learn. Her mind and heart were open in a way she had never experienced. That is what being in love will do. It has a silent language of its own that whispers its blessed intentions to the mind like a soft wind through the trees. It urges the body in expressions of care and desire. It speaks through one's eyes or the touch of a hand. Although Abby could not yet understand the language of the trees, she did perceive her heart's desire. Her love for Sherrod Dane was like a pre-written chapter that was meant to be discovered and inserted in the right place and time. The novel of her life would have been incomplete without it. Abby had thought that when she first saw his photograph. But she knew it for certain the day she met him in the meadow and looked into his hazel-blue eyes. The language of his heart had spoken to her. And she understood without question. Now there was a completeness within her, a vibrance to her life she had longed for. A wish had been granted, the result of a child's prayer.

Abby did not hear the sound of Sherrod's footsteps as he walked onto the porch. But she felt his presence and opened her eyes and smiled. "I thought about you all day," she said as Sherrod sat down close and faced her. The touch of his lips on hers thrilled her senses.

"And what did you decide?" His voice was just above a whisper. There was mint on his breath as he pushed back her hair and bit softly upon her earlobe. He traced the outline of her jaw with the fingers of his right hand, then gently kissed her neck.

Abby breathed in his scent of meadow flowers. She exhaled slowly. Her heart fluttered in anticipation. She combed her fingers through his hair and, finding his mouth with hers, she kissed him long and deep. "I've made no decision yet," she teased in a breathy voice. Playfully, she bit his lower lip. "But when I do, you'll be the first to know."

"Promise me?" Sherrod touched the top button of her blouse.

"Yes." Abby looked into his eyes as she answered. "I promise."

Neither one witnessed the sun's descent into the blue mountains, or even the first star that shone in the night sky. But when the moon found its place and the stars packed the heavens, Abby lay beneath them, naked and unashamed in the arms of the man who held her heart. "I love you, Sherrod." Her eyes were on the moon as she spoke, but her heart was in her words. "With my heart and soul, I do." She snuggled there in the warmth of his embrace while his heartbeat became her heartbeat.

A star arced across the sky, and Sherrod reached up and followed it with his hand. Then he kissed Abby's hair and said, *When I fell, the clouds parted and the sky shattered, sending splinters hot and cold through my heart. The earth opened, and I tumbled into its secrets where surrounded by silence, I found myself. I climbed again into the light, and there I saw your face, clear and gleaming in moonglow.*

Abby raised up and looked at Sherrod. Never had she heard such words. Never could she have imagined a soul such as his. Overcome with emotion, she could not speak.

Sherrod turned and leaned on his elbow. He took Abby's hand and held it to his cheek. *Feel me. My love is in the silence.* He touched his lips with her fingers. *Hear me. My voice is in the wind.* Then he placed her hand over his heart and pressed against it. *Know me. My devotion is forever.*

Abby could not hear the silent language of the

trees that night as they murmured among themselves. But there was not a doubt in her heart that love had found a voice in Sherrod Dane.

Emily Tynes heard the back door close, then the footsteps of her husband as he came down the hallway toward the den. She glanced in his direction as he entered just long enough to see the food tray he had brought in. "I'm not hungry, Doc," she said without looking up from her game of solitaire.

Doc stood there for a few silent seconds before he set the tray next to his and walked over to his wife. He bent over and touched her hand. "I'm not hungry, either, Em, but I do wish to talk with you."

Emily looked up. Instinctively, she knew the time had come for the one discussion they had avoided for years. Slowly she put away her cards. Doc sat down in his chair next to hers. A sad silence passed between the husband and wife before Doc cleared his throat and began. "Em, I don't know the right words to say, or even how to start this, but...."

For years Emily had waited for the day when finally the darkest secret of her husband's life, of her own life, would find its way into words. For so long, those words had not come from either of them. At first, they were not emotionally capable of speaking them. Words of admission and guilt. Accusations would have flowed into anger and hurt. Reasons, real and imagined, would have collided with blame and innuendo. Rumors would have coursed their way through the community, and lies would have spewed from unknowing lips. Innocence would have been lost and respect clouded.

Emily and Frank Tynes had not wanted that. They loved their home, their town, and its people. Their lives together. And so they had kept their secret. They kept it from the town and from each other. They thought they had even kept the secret from the secret. But mysteries, no matter how dark and hidden, have a way of coming to light.

Emily stopped her husband in mid-sentence with words he could not have imagined she would say. "I know the truth about Sherrod, Frank." There was no anger in her voice. No hint of blame or hatred. She had somehow shed herself of those feelings over the past weeks.

Doc was speechless for a minute. He bowed his head and stared at the carpet. Then he looked at Emily. "When did you know?" he asked.

Emily looked into Doc's hazel-blue eyes. "I knew the moment I saw his eyes," she answered.

Frank was a strong and quiet man. A lifetime of doctoring had rendered him emotionally aloof. But that night, he fell upon his knees and cried his heart out before the woman who knew his secret. Years of shame and guilt spilled from his heart as Emily knelt beside him and cradled him in her frail arms.

"God has punished me, Emily," he cried. "Every day I've walked in the shame of my unfaithfulness. So dark," he sobbed. "God, it's been so dark. My soul." Doc clinched his fists in agony and pushed away.

Emily did not ask if he had been in love with Laura Dane. She did not have to. Years ago, she had seen the framed pictures in the cabin. She had seen the look in Laura's eyes. She knew that look. And she knew who had taken the photographs. She could not imagine the pain and guilt of being in love with two people at the same time. But she knew it did happen. It had happened to her husband. And it had torn their hearts. Her decision to live with it was not one most women would have made. But it was her decision and her heart. It was also her faith that allowed her to live with the truth of it. She had loved Frank Tynes since she was a schoolgirl. She could not stop loving him and could not imagine her life without him. Emily knew he had never stopped loving her.

Sherrod was a love child, but he was also the son she could not have. He had the eyes of his father. How could she not love him also? How could she not forgive?

"Look at me, Frank." Emily wiped away her own tears. Her voice was gentle.

"I can't." Doc did not look up as he responded.

"Look in my eyes, Frank." Emily placed her hand on Doc's cheek.

"I can't look into your eyes, just as I can't look into Sherrod's. My shame won't allow it."

Emily cupped Doc's face in her hands. "These are the same eyes that loved you when I was young. These are the eyes of the woman who married you and loves you beyond your mistakes."

Doc looked at his wife. Tears welled in her eyes. He watched her put her hand to her heart, and he finally understood the depth of her love when she said, "This is the heart that forgives you. I think God already has."

Later that night, Doc helped Emily into bed and just before he turned off the light, he asked, "What about Sherrod?"

Emily smiled. She reached over and touched a spray of wild flowers Sherrod had brought to her. "Sherrod is our son."

"But what should I say to him?"

Emily found Doc's hand and squeezed it. "If anyone knows the truth, it's Sherrod. I don't think you need to say but one word."

Doc kissed his wife and turned out the light.

"Listen to the wind outside, Frank," Emily said sleepily. "The trees are dancing."

Charles Pauley pulled his truck into Dan Glass's service station, parked and listened to the weather forecast on the radio before he turned off the engine. A cold front was moving in. "That oughta bring some thunder boomers," he said to no one in particular as he stepped out of the truck.

"Hey, Charley," a familiar voice called. Charles looked and saw Ed Conner standing at the front door of the station, beside Dan.

"Well, I'll be," Charles spoke as he walked over to his old friend. "Ed, what in the world are you doing over here?" He reached out his hand. "A little off your beat, aren't you?"

Ed, a tall, thin, man in his early sixties, smiled and shook Charles' hand. "It's good to see you, Charley. Retirement has been good to you."

Charles laughed and patted his round stomach. "A little too good, Ed."

"Shirley feeds him pretty good," Dan entered the conversation. "And if she didn't keep him on-the-go all the time, he'd be bigger than both of us put together."

The men chuckled. A car pulled up at the gas pumps and Dan excused himself.

"What's going on, Ed?" Charles was curious. It was his nature. "You just passin' through, or what?"

Ed scratched his neck and looked over at Dan, who had just pulled up the hood of the car he was servicing. "I'm looking for a man that goes by the name of Nash Moseley."

Charles clinched his teeth and shook his head. "I can't say I'm surprised. He's a bad one."

"What do you know about him?" Ed asked while thumbing through a notepad with the eraser of his pencil. "Dan tells me you two had words a few weeks ago."

Charles folded his arms over his chest and grimaced. "Yeah. He caused a bit of a scene not far from here, and I told him to back off."

Ed found his place in his notes. "That would have been a verbal confrontation with Sherrod Dane?"

"Yep. There was a gathering of folks up in the meadow, and Sherrod, well…."

"He's some sort of healer, right?" Ed was referring to his notes and did not look at Charles when he interrupted with his question.

Charles did not hesitate with his response. "Sherrod Dane is what he is, Ed. And folks around here think an awful lot of him, too." Charles looked up at the mountain, then back at his friend. "Anyway, Nash starts smartin' off with him, and some of the men there were about to do something about it until Sherrod stopped them. Nash quieted down after that but stuck around until the gathering broke up. Later, I saw him at his car and told him to back off. But he pretty much ignored me. That's the last I've seen of him. I heard he lost his job over at the bottle company a few days later. I thought he had left town."

Ed wrote down some notes on his pad and then stuffed it in his coat pocket.

"What has he done, Ed?" Charles' voice was low.

Ed sighed and shook his head. Charles noticed his hair was much grayer than it was the last time they had met. Creases on his forehead were more defined. His eyes, sunken and dark. All were signs of the stress of the job that few would envy. Ed Conner was a long-time investigator for the Roanoke County Sheriff's department. He had held the job for over twenty years. Due to his own past career in law enforcement, Charles Pauley knew all too well the sinister side of human nature that Ed had seen.

"We've connected him with the disappearances

of two women over in Roanoke last year, and three others." Ed looked over at Dan, who was talking with his customer. Then he added quietly, "One young girl was a student at UVA, then there was a housewife in Lexington, and an elderly woman over in Nelson County."

"All of them still missing?" Charles asked.

"We found the housewife and the older woman." Ed looked down at the pavement as he answered. "They were, well...," Ed paused to find the words to express the visions in his mind. "Put it this way, Charley. Death had to be a blessing, after what they had been through."

Charles shook his head. "I knew he was a bad one, but I didn't figure on something like this. Do you know where he's from?"

"We've got a team of investigators putting this thing together now. It seems Moseley was born into a pretty nice family in a little town in Pennsylvania but has been trouble from the get-go. No one knew what his problem was. He left home early. A drifter." Ed finished as Dan approached.

"That's Tom Jordan's wife, Mary, just pulling away." Dan nodded his head toward her car as she drove out onto the street. "She says Tom told her that Moseley bought a hunting knife and some rope from him a few days after he was fired from his job."

Ed Conner watched Mary Jordan's car disappear down the street. "Where's the hardware store, Dan?" he asked.

"Right in the middle of town."

"You think Tom is there now?"

Dan looked at his wristwatch. "I think you can catch him if you leave now."

Ed patted Dan on the arm. "I'm going to head on over there. Thanks."

"You bet, Ed." Dan walked back into the station.

Charles walked with Ed over to his car. "What do you think, Ed? Do you think he's still around here?"

Ed opened his car door and turned to Charles. "From what I can tell, he's a real mixed bag. He's a stalker and an opportunist. No woman is really safe around him, and if he focuses on one, he's going to stay close and put in the time it takes to get her alone." Ed sat behind the steering wheel of his car and started the engine. "I don't know where he is, Charley, but if he did buy a knife and some rope, he's got somebody on his mind. My gut tells me he's still close by." Ed closed the door and rolled down his window. "You take care, Charley. And if you see or hear anything, give me a call. I'm heading over to the hardware store."

Charles tapped Ed's car roof with his hand and waved. "I will, Ed." He watched Ed leave and then looked up at the mountain. That day in the meadow was still fresh in his mind. It worried him. A man like Nash Moseley did not just show up for something like that. There was a reason he had come to the meadow that day.

Charles was so close to the answer, and although he had seen the reason for Nash's presence in the meadow, he had not recognized it. Even Sherrod Dane, a man who had the power to look into men's souls, had not fully understood Nash's purpose. A glimpse was all Nash had allowed Sherrod, but in that instant, he had recognized Nash as a dark heart—one ruled by evil. Sherrod had seen them before, along with the tempters. He was always on guard against them. He and those like him who walked in the truth and light of the good spirit were targets. But there were others in danger, for evil knows no boundaries and feeds on the vulnerable. Nash Moseley was a clever dark heart. He prided himself on it.

"What was he like when he was a boy, Doc?" Abby sat in a chair across from Doc in the den, days after Doc and Emily had had their talk. The good smells from the kitchen told her that supper was almost ready.

Doc smiled. "Well, he didn't use the door often. He'd climb that big walnut tree up to the roof and go in his bedroom window."

"Did he ever say why he did that?" Abby wanted to know all she could about the man she loved. Sherrod had told her so much, but there were still questions it would take a lifetime together to answer.

"He just said he liked to climb trees. Jesse Lou and Henri used to leave his lunch at the base of the big magnolia in the back yard. He would be sitting on a limb in the top of it, just listening." Doc shook his head in wonder as he recalled. "I would ask him what he was listening for, and he'd say, 'Anything they wish to tell me.'"

"Did you believe him?" Abby stood up and walked over to the den window.

"I have always believed Sherrod," Doc answered. "Even when he has told me things I didn't want to hear."

Abby looked over at Doc with a compassionate expression on her face. "You mean Emily?"

Doc got up and walked over and stood next to Abby. "Sherrod knew even before she was diagnosed. He knew what she had, and he knows when it will take her away." Doc looked out into the evening shadows. "Of all his gifts, that is one I do not envy."

Abby leaned her head against Frank's shoulder. "He'll be here soon, Doc."

Doc put his arm around Abby. "My light in the darkness, Abby. He was that as a child, and he is as a man." He squeezed her gently.

"I love him, Doc." Abby softly voiced her admission.

Doc smiled. "We know you do."

"Is it that obvious?"

"Like an open book," Doc chuckled. "Emily and I think it is wonderful. He squeezed Abby's shoulder. "Now, let's go into the kitchen and see what delicious dishes the gals are serving up tonight."

At about the same time, Emily heard a thud on the porch roof outside her bedroom window. She rose from her chair and waited. In a moment, she reached down and picked up a thin, white shawl from the arm of her chair, and when she looked up, Sherrod was standing beside the open window. "There you are," she said while pulling the shawl over her narrow shoulders. "Abby is downstairs with Doc."

"I know." Sherrod walked over to the woman and hugged her gently.

"Where did you go?"

Sherrod stepped back and offered Emily a pale lavender flower. "I had to go far away this time, Em."

Emily took the flower and gently laced it into the weave of her shawl. "And how did it turn out?" she asked.

Sherrod walked over to the bedside table and touched Emily's Bible with his fingers. "I could help to ease the pain of a child, Em. But I could not save her." There was such sadness in his voice.

Emily understood. She had heard those words time and again from him. Such was the life of Sherrod Dane. So gifted. So powerful. And yet so helpless when faced with the journey of the soul. She could only imagine the sorrow his heart had known at times. "It's God's will, Sherrod, to move the spirit onward and closer to His kingdom."

"I know." Sherrod looked into Emily's eyes. "But sometimes I wish that I could halt it just for a little while." He could see Emily's fading spirit. "I want to hold you here with me and Doc. I want you to see my happiness with Abby." Sherrod fought back his tears as he continued. "I know more than anyone about how it all works. About the spirit's journey back to the light. But I am not yet ready to let you go. You have been my mother and my dear friend when you could have turned your face from me and hated my existence. It is true, Em. And I know the truth. Even if it is not spoken. I know it. I have seen my father's eyes."

Emily took Sherrod's hands in hers. She squeezed them and said, "Listen to me, Sherrod. You were born of love. I know that in my heart. I knew when I first laid eyes on you and held you in my arms. You are the son I could not conceive with my body. Yet you were brought to me to love and cherish. A gift from God, and with the eyes of your father. If I can accept this and believe it with my heart and soul, then so must you." Emily allowed Sherrod to look deeply into her soul. "As for saving me, I think we both already know that I am saved. That is not a worry for you. Just know this: It is through you and your father that I have learned that the greatest gift is to love and be loved. And the greatest task is to forgive." Emily embraced her son and spoke secretively. "Jonathan told me that something good has happened."

Sherrod looked toward the window at the leafy branches of the old walnut tree. "What did that old tree spirit have to say?" he asked.

"Just that the trees have been dancing under the moon and stars since two hearts became one." Emily was coy. "Of course, it could just be tree gibberish, I guess."

Sherrod smiled and shook his head. "It is time to go downstairs, Em. Doc and Abby are waiting."

The Tynes' dining room was filled with much talk and laughter that evening. Abby had never seen Emily so animated. And Doc was full of stories she had never heard. He told of beautiful trout streams and places deep in the mountains where he and Sherrod had walked to in years past. She listened to Doc's voice and its inflections. She noticed even more his smile. She noticed his hazel-blue eyes and wondered how anyone could not know the truth. Or was the secret kept by the entire community? If the truth was known, then it was unspoken. A silent alliance born of respect.

Abby knew the truth. It had not taken her long to suspect it. It did, however, take her some time to understand how the family had lived with it. Something had changed. Abby could tell. She saw the results. Doc and Emily were closer, perhaps returning to the way they had been before. And Sherrod, the quiet and faithful son, the special one who had brought both joy and pain to their hearts, was in this home again.

Abby had found a family. She had come into it at the right time and moved it forward in ways she could not have known.

Sherrod held her hand underneath the table and leaned over to her. "Are you sure?" he asked.

"You know I am," she answered. Her eyes sparkled. Sherrod cleared his throat and summoned Jesse Lou and Henri from the kitchen. Doc and Emily were quiet, but their eyes showed their anticipation.

"Doc and Em, Jesse Lou and Henri." Sherrod looked at each individual as he called their names. "I love this woman." He looked adoringly at Abby as he spoke. "And she has said she will marry me in the meadow when the leaves begin to turn in the fall."

Tears of joy filled the eyes of everyone in the room that night. But Sherrod and Abby were the happiest of all.

Dora Lindstrom trusted people too often. It was her weakness, the one thing she could not change about her character. Two failed marriages and a dozen romantic relationships had not changed her. Nor had the advice of her two grown sons from her first marriage. They worried that she was gullible and an easy mark for someone with evil intent. They lived away and had a right to worry. It is a shame they did not live closer to their mother, or that they did not drive along Route 60 between Lexington and Buena Vista more often. If they had, perhaps one of them would have been there the evening her back tire blew out, and she struggled to replace it with a spare. They would not have needed the help of a stranger. They might have seen something in his eyes that their mother could not see. But life has variables which bring about turns. Some of those turns are good, and some are bad. But few are foreseen.

Dora was glad to see the stranger who stopped and offered to change her tire. Her job search in Lexington had not gone well, and the flat tire was the cap on her day of rejection. The stranger's kindness and know-how seemed genuine, and Dora welcomed it. The conversation was pleasant but, as always, the attractive, middle-aged woman divulged too much about herself. She should have never mentioned that she lived alone. She should have never accepted the stranger's offer to follow her home to make sure the old spare tire survived the trip. But Dora was a trusting person, and she took him at his word. That was a shame. Dora could not have made a worse decision.

Nash Moseley stepped out of the shower and dried off his body with a fresh-smelling towel. He swiped the towel across the medicine cabinet mirror and looked at his misty reflection. He shaved, rinsed, and dried his face. It felt good to be clean after days of living in his car and sleeping on back roads. The last forty-eight hours had been good for him. Food and a comfortable bed to sleep in. He had indulged in the comforts he missed. He walked out of the bathroom and down the hallway to the bedroom door which was ajar. He tapped on the door with his fingernails. "Dora, I'm back," he said teasingly. He pushed open the door and walked into the darkened room. The sound of her fast breathing brought a cruel smile to his lips. His heartbeat became faster as he walked over to the bed and turned on the lamp. He arranged framed pictures of Dora's children and young grandchildren so that she could see them. Then he pulled the sheet back, exposing her nudity. "I'm glad you waited for me," he said, eyeing the ropes that bound her wrists and ankles to the corners of the bed. "But then, you weren't going anywhere anyway, were you?"

Dora's eyes were wide with terror. She struggled helplessly. She had never known evil until she accepted help from this stranger. Since then, the humiliation and violation she had been put through were unimaginable. She gazed at the photos of her family, then closed her eyes and turned her face away from them. "Please don't kill me," she begged in a trembling whisper.

Nash crawled into the bed and touched her neck with the tip of his hunting knife. She winced and whimpered. He lowered his face to the woman's ear and whispered, "Not yet, Dora."

It is not very hard to tell where evil will manifest itself. It moves in and out of man's consciousness. It takes hold in willing and vulnerable minds. Scientists want to blame one's evil actions on how one is brought up. That assumption has its merits. But Nash Moseley came from a good family who offered him every advantage in life, and look what happened. True evil is predestined. It chooses its vessel carefully. It hovers over the womb like a thundercloud ready to burst. And once it falls, it guides every step of its chosen one.

Dora Lindstrom was a good woman. A trusting woman. It was that trust that blinded her to the evil intent of Nash Moseley. That is what killed her.

It was one in the morning before Abby finally stopped writing and closed the hardbound journal that contained the novel she was creating. The words and ideas had come easily. The story was flowing. Abby was happy. She had read somewhere that the really good stories wrote themselves. She was beginning to believe that. Her own life's story was writing itself. She was conscious of that. Every step of her life, every trial and triumph had led to where she was. It all seemed like part of a large plan, an evolving story in which her character was swept along by some mysterious hand. She was growing in mind and spirit. Everything she dreamed of seemed possible to her. She was in love. And it was right. Abby had met her soul mate in Sherrod. There was no doubt in her mind. She knew it before she had even met him. Who could understand that? The first time she lay eyes on his photograph and heard his name, she knew. Abby's life story was indeed writing itself, and her part was to listen to her heart and follow it.

Distant thunder sounded over the mountains, and Abby got up from her chair and walked through the house to the front door. She opened it and looked out into the woods past the yard. The wind was steady and damp. She thought about Sherrod out on a night like this. She wondered if he was ever frightened in the darkness and the vastness of the mountains he roamed. She saw the sky light up beyond the mountains to the west. She contemplated walking up to his cabin to wait for him. He would certainly be home soon. Her wristwatch showed almost two o'clock a.m. Something had kept him longer than he had planned. He walked slower at night. Three mountains away was much farther than it seemed. The path was winding.

There were streams to ford and steep inclines to traverse. He could have driven his truck along narrow dirt roads to get to the one who needed him, but he preferred the walk under the trees. He had told her that he walked whenever he could so that he could listen to what nature had to say to him. It was Abby's love for Sherrod that allowed her to accept what she could not understand about him.

She closed the front door but did not lock it. She felt safe so close to Sherrod. Her door was always open to him, and his to her. It was a lovers' arrangement.

Abby walked back into her bedroom and opened her closet door. She brought out one of Sherrod's white linen shirts and held it to her face. She could smell his scent on it. She undressed and put on the shirt. She slept in it whenever he was not there.

Abby was tired. She thought back over her day as she strummed chords on the Martin guitar Sherrod had insisted she keep with her. It had been a busy morning at Doc's office with walk-in patients. Then she had accompanied Doc on several house calls in the afternoon. After supper, she had talked at length with Emily about the upcoming wedding. It was almost dark when she had finally said goodbye and started home. She had listened to the car radio and knew that a severe thunderstorm watch was in the forecast. Abby put her guitar down and walked over to the window. The thunder was still distant, but the breeze that swelled the curtains against her body was cooler than before. She buttoned her shirt and closed the window. She said a prayer and wished that Sherrod was with her.

It's funny how most childhood fears fade away with age. Abby had always been afraid of storms. Why? She did not know. Perhaps it was the unbridled rage a storm could bring with it, or its humbling power over every living and man-made thing.

The sky lit up, and Abby closed her eyes to her fear. She pushed away the premonition that told her this storm was different from any she had ever known.

Days before, Nash Moseley had hidden his black Bel Air in a rickety abandoned tobacco barn at the end of a grown-over dirt road off Route 60, three miles west of Buena Vista. It was not far from Dora Lindstrom's house. He had walked under the cover of darkness back to Dora's place and buried her body in a shallow grave in the woods, then he had taken her car and her money. Instinct told him to be careful. He hid during the day and moved at night, watching and waiting for the opportunity to carry out his evil desire. He knew he should leave the area for good. But he could not get Abby Rhode out of his mind. He was obsessed with her to the point where his survival skills were hindered. He was used to drifting freely from place to place. But now he was like a cat waiting for its prey.

And finally, the time had come. The evenings of parking Dora's car at the end of Chestnut Avenue and waiting and watching for the opportunity to follow

Abby had paid off. He now knew where she lived. It was perfect. The little house beside Indian Gap Run was isolated, and she was alone. But Nash did not know everything. There had not been time. Too much was coming in on him. The hiding during the day was hindering his freedom to move about and learn what was being said in the town and if the law was honing in on him. There was not enough time to properly stalk Abby.

Nash followed Abby as she left the Tynes residence just before dark. There was thunder in the distance beyond the mountains as he pulled off Indian Gap trace and onto a weedy path that led beneath some low-branched dogwoods. There he left the car and walked through the woods until he came to the small, wood-frame house built years before by Woodrow Marsden. The lights were on when he arrived, and he walked around the house, casing it. He caught glimpses of Abby going from room to room and finally settling at her desk, where she sat and wrote in a book for hours. He stood close at the window and watched her every move. Thoughts, dark and cruel, crossed his mind. He wanted to take her with him. He wanted to possess her and rule her every breath. But he knew better. He could tell that day at the church and later in the meadow that he would have no chance with Abby. She would never willingly accept him. He would have to take her, and he was ready.

For hours he watched. He had to control himself from almost running up on the front porch when she stood there at the open door. He did not know what she was thinking. He did not know that she was waiting for someone. He did not care. His heart pounded in his chest when he saw her undress. And when she walked to the window and the wind blew back her unbuttoned shirt, his mouth watered. Still he waited. He waited until long after she turned out her bedroom light. And when the thunder rolled over the mountain, he stepped up on the front porch and turned the doorknob.

A bolt of lightning stripped the bark from a tall pine tree and blasted a hole at its base in the yard of Charles and Shirley Pauley.

Charles was on his feet in seconds.

"Did it hit the house, honey?" Shirley sat up in bed, switched on the bedside lamp and watched her husband pull on his robe. The light flickered.

"No. I think it got a tree at the edge of the yard, though." Charles started out of the bedroom. "You go on back to sleep. I'm just going to take a look around."

Shirley snuggled back under the covers but left on the light. She looked at the alarm clock. It was three-thirty a.m.

Charles opened the kitchen door and looked outside. He could smell fresh pine bark. The air smelled like a pulpwood yard. Heavy rain began to fall, and the wind swept it toward him. He closed the door and walked over to the telephone, where he fumbled through a wooden box until he brought out a card with a name and number on it. He picked up the phone and dialed the number. The pops and crackles on the line hurt his ears, and he held the receiver inches away.

A sleepy and half-annoyed greeting came on the third ring.

"Hello, Ed? This is Charles Pauley, over in Buena Vista."

Ed Conner cleared his throat. "Yeah, Charley. What in the world is going on?"

"Look, Ed, we've got a bad storm over here right now, and I can't talk long. But I've been thinking about what you said about Nash Moseley staying around this area for some reason."

There was a loud pop over the phone line.

"What do you know, Charley?" Ed became alert and was very interested.

"Well, I got a feeling I know who he's after."

Ed seemed confused. "Charley, I don't think he's gonna go after Dane." Ed knew all about the confrontation in the meadow between Nash and Sherrod. "He's trouble for everybody, but he targets women."

"I don't think it's Sherrod, Ed. I think it's the young woman he's going to marry."

"Who's that?" Ed asked.

Lightning struck again, and a loud pop and crackle over the phone line forced Charles to put down the receiver. He walked back into the bedroom and started dressing.

"What are you doing, Charles?" Shirley was standing beside the bed, a puzzled look on her face.

Charles buckled his belt and pulled on his shoes. "I've got a bad feeling, Shirley. Remember that Sunday at church when we saw Nash Moseley leaning in the window of the Tynes' car?"

Shirley walked around the foot of the bed and stood next to her husband. "Yes. That was odd," she recalled.

Charles stood up. "Yes, it was," he agreed. "And then he was so angry he just about ran over old man Cabell and his wife as they walked across the road."

Shirley remembered. "What are you onto?"

Charles put on his jacket and hat. He walked over to the bedside table and pulled out the drawer.

Shirley put her hand to her mouth as she watched him load the thirty-eight caliber handgun he had owned for years.

"Good heavens, Charles! Tell me."

Charles put the loaded gun in a clip holster and hung it on his belt. "Well, that day in the meadow, Abby Rhode was nervous. She kept looking past me while I was talking to her and Sherrod." Charles placed his hands on his wife's shoulders and looked directly into her eyes. "I know fear when I see it, Shirley. And that girl was scared to death of someone. And that someone was Nash Moseley. He was standing on the hillside behind me. I just know he followed her up there. He's a killer, Shirley. Probably has done it more than once. Ed Conner thinks he's still here, and I got a strong feeling I know what he wants."

Shirley was frightened. "Charles, please wait and get Ed in on this. You're too old to be going out like this."

Charles Pauley's mind was set. "Once a lawman, always a lawman. You know that." He turned to leave the bedroom. "Now, you get on the phone to Doc Tynes and tell him I'm on my way over to pick him up."

"Well, isn't Abby over there?" Shirley did not know Abby had moved.

"She's living alone up at the old Marsden's place," Charles answered.

Shirley followed her husband into the kitchen. She picked up the phone and dialed the Tynes' number. "Why now, Charles?" she asked as Charles opened the door to leave. "Why do you think something is going to happen now?"

"I don't know that it will. But we gotta get that girl to a safe place until Moseley is caught." Charles closed the door behind him as he stepped out into the storm.

A second later, Frank Tynes picked up on the other end of the phone line. Shirley Pauley could hardly contain her emotions as she began explaining.

Sherrod had barely stepped a foot into his cabin when the rain began to fall in earnest. Heavy droplets blew in thick sheets against the window panes. The thunder rolled across the sky like giant bowling balls. Its rumbling shook the foundation of the cabin. Brilliant and jagged bolts of cloud-to-ground lightning filled the sky and threatened the earth. The mantle clock chimed. It was three-forty-five a.m.

Sherrod had stayed too long at the Clifford home, miles away over the mountains. He should have driven. He had known a storm was coming. He knew that Abby was afraid of storms. But he was not used to curfews or deadlines. He was used to going where he was needed, and although he often rushed to get there, he seldom hurried to get back home. There were always delays. Always things to see. People to meet. And there were the trees, the silent ones who spoke mostly to him when he walked unhurriedly among them. But that night, he did not listen to them. There was no time for it. He had accepted the invitation to stay at the Clifford's home after having healed John Clifford of a shoulder injury he had incurred from a fall out of a fruit tree. But by two o'clock a.m., Sherrod was restless and left for home. He wanted to be with Abby and would have gone down to her house if he could have gotten there ahead of the storm. But the trace he had followed over and around the mountains was winding and treacherous. He moved through dark woods slowly and carefully. The sound of the howling wind through the passes made it impossible for him to hear the language of the trees. Although he did feel the need to go home, he did not perceive a danger beyond that which is common with a thunderstorm.

Had it been quieter, he would have known for sure that something was wrong.

Sherrod looked again at the mantle clock. He wanted to continue down the mountain and across the meadow. He wanted to sleep in the arms of his wife-to-be. He walked out on the porch and sat down in a rocking chair. He decided to wait instead for the storm to ease. Then he would go to her and wake her with a kiss. The wind was so loud. Sherrod closed his eyes and waited.

From the instant Abby closed her eyes, sleep came in intervals interrupted by long, angry rumblings and earth-shaking crashes. She would open her eyes to flashes of white light that filled her bedroom. Her sleep was fitful at best, and she was frightened more than usual. There was something troubling her deep inside, a confused warning of impending danger. Was it the storm? She wondered. Was it that she worried about Sherrod? He was all right. She knew he was. Sherrod was in his element.

A deafening explosion pounded the sky above her house and practically shook her out of bed. She jumped to her feet and, off balance, fell against the wall next to the window. Streaks of lightning flashed across the bedroom, and in a speck of a second, she saw the figure of a man at the bedroom door.

"Sherrod?"

Another flash of lightning. The figure moved enough for Abby to see that it was not Sherrod. A chill came over Abby as she stood up and watched in horror as the figure rushed toward her in blinding white strobes of light. His eyes were wide and as black as a bottomless pit. His yellow and stained teeth were bared behind a maniacal smile. A blade flashed in his hand as he lunged at her.

Abby pushed away from the wall and jumped over the bed, falling hard against her chest of drawers. Nash Moseley jammed his fingers against the wall and cursed. He turned and jumped over the bed. Abby kicked at him, but he kicked back, the toe of his shoe sinking into her abdomen. Breathless, she curled into a fetal position, pulling the night stand on top of her and using it as a shield. Nash kicked and stomped at her furiously, breaking the wooden night stand into pieces over her body. Then he reached down and, grabbing a handful of her hair, pulled Abby up and slammed her head into the wall. She was stunned by the blow and felt the helplessness of her situation as Nash's enraged power picked her up and hurled her back over the bed. Instinctively, she lifted herself up just as Nash jerked her to her feet by her hair and pushed her face down onto the bed. He jammed his knee between her legs and pressed his hand down hard on the back of her neck. The pain was excruciating, but Abby did not cry out. Nash leaned forward until his lips were touching her ear. She could feel the heat of his breath and smell its foulness. "That's it," he said in a breathy rasp. "Just lay still, and I won't slit your sweet skin." He licked her cheek and touched her temple with the point of his knife.

Abby did not move. But her mind did not stop. She waited. Like a snake, she would strike. Her heart beat loudly into the bed's mattress as Nash lessened his grip on her neck. "Now, real easy, you're gonna turn over on your back. I want to see your face." He laid his knife's edge against her neck and leaned to the side, withdrawing his knee. "Turn over!" he demanded.

Abby felt the pressure of the blade against her skin as she obeyed.

Outside the storm continued to rage. The constant strobe of light from the electrically charged air allowed Nash to feast his eyes on his prey, his lust for her heightened by her vulnerability. He thrust his knee between her legs again and smiled viciously. *This was worth waiting for,* he thought as he pulled at the top button of her shirt and severed its stitch with the blade of his knife. "One," he said smiling. "Don't you move." He touched her throat with the tip of the knife and slowly ran it down her skin to the second button. "Two." He snapped the button off and with the tip of the blade pushed open her shirt, exposing one breast. He licked his lips with his tongue as his breathing became heavier.

Abby did not move. She waited, staring into the blackness of his eyes. This was true evil. This was what Sherrod had told her existed in the world. A cruelty beyond imagination. Madder than a rabid dog. A consuming force, ravenous in nature.

"You and your kind," he growled with clinched teeth. "Don't you move until I tell you to."

Nash ran his coarse fingers along the outside of Abby's thigh. Her skin was like satin, cool and smooth. He pushed up her shirt and placed his hand on her stomach. Her jaw tightened with disgust. He swallowed and reached for his belt.

At that moment a blinding flash of lightning struck close to the house with an immediate thunderous crash which shook everything. That is when Abby struck with all her might, her knee coming up hard between Nash's legs. The force of her kick sent him sprawling into the floor at the foot of the bed, where he writhed, coughing and moaning.

Abby fled out of the bedroom and ran out the front door before Nash could get to his feet. A flash of lightning showed him his knife, and he grabbed it and, cursing, stumbled after her.

It was still dark and storming even in the pre-dawn hour when Nash raced out the front door and glimpsed Abby's escape across the narrow foot bridge and up the driveway. A bolt of lightning struck nearby, and thunder shook the earth as he began to chase after her. But still he could hear her cry out a name above the storm. It was a name he had heard before. A name whose owner he despised by his nature. He had heard Abby say it when he was at her bedroom door earlier. So Sherrod Dane was her lover!

Nash screamed a curse and ran after Abby with renewed conviction.

Sherrod opened his eyes and stood up. The porch floorboards vibrated beneath his feet with the thunder that rolled out of a sudden and horrendous crash. He walked to the edge of the porch and listened intensely. There was something beyond the thunder. Something that piqued his senses. A cry. His name. Abby's voice. Was it just a dream? He had been tired and had closed his eyes. He must have drifted off. That was it. A dream. He leaned out and looked up past the canopy of trees. Dawn was struggling with the raging darkness. Lightning flashed, and thunder pounded like bombs in a blitz. Rain fell in torrents.

Sherrod wiped his face with his hand. The wind shifted, and a cold, wet gust swept onto the porch. A rocking chair blew over. Ferns that Abby had potted and placed at the top of the porch steps tumbled, their fronds submerging in the rippling puddle of water that had collected on the walkway. Shards of broken clay littered the flat, stone steps.

Sherrod balanced himself by holding onto a porch post. It was as if the wind were pulling him away. And then he heard it again. A cry between a crack of lightning and the loud boom that followed it. That was no dream. He turned his face toward the meadow and cleared the steps in a single bound. His acute senses were heightened as he sprinted among the trees and rocks. The bending trees urged him forward, cautioning him of danger. He listened as best he could, but the storm was so loud it would not allow him to hear everything.

The rain pelted his face and soaked his body. His heart pounded as he raced toward the meadow. "Abby!" he cried out loud. A fear that he had never known groped at his heart, but he would not allow it to take hold. There was no time for fear. No time for caution. There was only Abby. He knew that above all. So he ran. He ran like the wind that whipped the treetops, through a storm that would have blinded most men and sent them cowering for shelter. He ran without concern for himself, for in nature, Sherrod Dane feared nothing.

Stones cut Abby's bare feet as she ran across the road and up the winding pathway through the woods toward the meadow. A bolt of lightning and a crash of thunder caused her to bend low but did not halt her speed. She heard Nash's voice when he cried out after her, but she did not look back. And when she entered the meadow, she did not know how close behind her he was. Abby's mind was set on getting to Sherrod. Halfway across the meadow she called out his name again. That was just before she tripped over a hidden rock. Her body flipped through the air, and she landed hard and skidded through the wet clover. When she stopped, she glanced at her left foot. Her toes were bleeding and numb. She raised up and searched frantically through the blowing sheets of rain. Finally she made out the form of Nash running across the meadow. She turned and continued her escape.

Nash did not see Abby. He could not be sure where she would enter the woods on the other side. But he did have an idea where Sherrod's cabin might be located. He remembered where Sherrod appeared from out of the woods on the afternoon he had followed Abby there. He was too worked up to stop now. He was too full of rage and lust to turn back. A tree hugger did not scare him. Nash felt invincible. He hated Sherrod Dane. He knew that the first time he had heard of him. The respect and protection afforded the so-called healer on the mountain by the people of Buena Vista only deepened Nash's loathing of him. He was born to hate Sherrod and anyone like him. But now that hate had grown even more sinister. To think that there was something between Abby and Sherrod fueled the torch inside of Nash. He should have seen it that day in the meadow. If he'd had more time, he would have. But things had gotten out of hand. His ego had grown too large. He had said too much. Crossed too many lives in the town. That thing with the Borden girl had brought attention to him that he did not need. He had become cocky and mouthy. He should have honed in on Abby early on and then hit the road. That was his way. Stay quiet and watchful. Get close and plan. Then carry out and leave. But things were catching up with Nash, and he could not leave yet. The storm was a good cover. There was still time to take what he wanted.

Nash could barely make out the big tree where Sherrod had stood the day he appeared in the meadow. He ran to it. Breathing heavily, he leaned against it searching with wide eyes into the grayness of the forest. He was about to step into the woods when a movement caught his attention. He blinked his eyes and wiped the rainwater from his face with his shirt sleeve. When he looked again, he realized a figure wearing white was approaching fast through the trees. He remembered Sherrod Dane wearing a white shirt. He could not believe his luck. This was the tree hugger coming to Abby's rescue. He knew it. Nash noticed a narrow path that Sherrod would follow into the meadow. Slowly, he crept behind a thick pine tree. Once in position, he readied himself, knife in hand.

Abby ran wildly through the forest toward Sherrod's cabin, missing the path completely. If she had only entered the woods farther down the meadow, she would have met him. But there was too much confusion. The rain was so heavy, and her fall had thrown her off.

Sherrod could see the opening at the edge of the woods as he leaped over a fallen branch and rounded a bend in the path. His eyes were scanning the edges of the meadow when a dark figure stepped out from behind a tree, and he slammed into it, feeling its strong grip around his waist. Shots of pain seared through his body as he fell and slid over wet leaves, mud and stones. When he came to rest, Sherrod lay on his back at the edge of the forest. He tried, but could not move for the weight on top of him. He opened his eyes and in an extended flash of lightning saw the face of Nash Moseley. It did not take two seconds to see the evil he had suspected in the man.

Nash's face hovered close as he pressed his knife to its hilt between Sherrod's ribs. He rubbed Sherrod's face with a muddy hand and pushed off him into a crouching position. Rainwater dripped from his nose as he looked down at Sherrod's bloody shirt. "I got you four times there, tree hugger." Nash pulled the hunting knife out of Sherrod's body and wiped it in the wet leaves beside his head. He bent forward and with a cruel smile snorted, "Heal that."

Sherrod could not move. But he could hear and see. And he could feel the life draining from his body.

Nash stood up and peered up the path. "Well, I'd love to just stay here and watch you die, tree hugger, but I got a date. Don't worry. I'll come back to bury you." He stepped over Sherrod's body and looked down at him. "Just wait til I tell Abby who I ran into."

Sherrod watched Nash turn and leave. For a moment, he lay still. Then he dug his heels into the earth and pushed himself closer to the oak tree. His pain was excruciating, but he did not stop until his head was propped against the bowl of the tree. It was an effort, but he managed to lift his hands enough to tear open his shirt. Blood oozed from his wounds. He felt as if his head were swimming in and out of consciousness. The rain intensified, and it felt cool on his skin. Sherrod turned his head to the side and focused his eyes on a pale and delicate flower that grew at the tree's base. "We stand strong in the storm, little flower. Faith," he whispered.

Voices came like waves into his mind as he lay there. Words unspoken yet understood. The silent language. Sherrod slowly reached his hand over and touched a petal of the flower. Then he laid one hand upon the root of the tree and reached up and called out, "God, help me!"

Deafening thunder pounded the earth and long bolts of lightning split the sky.

Charles Pauley had never seen a storm of such intensity. He hurried from around the back of Abby's house and met Frank Tynes on the front porch. "Nothing around back, Doc," he called out.

Doc's eyes were wide with fear. "There's been a struggle in there, Charley!" he shouted.

Charles came up to the porch. "Abby's car is still parked in the driveway, and Sherrod's truck is in the garage." He thought for a second. "The front door was wide open. I think she ran. She didn't have time to get in the car and drive off."

Doc looked up the driveway. "She'd run to Sherrod, Charley. If she got away, she'd try to get to him. Let's go!"

Abby flung open the cabin door and ran upstairs, screaming Sherrod's name. When she saw that his bed had not been slept in, she realized he had not come home. She ran back downstairs and saw Nash crossing the front yard. Terrified, she slammed the front door and locked it.

Nash did not hesitate at the door and kicked it off its hinges with ease. He entered the cabin like one possessed of a demon, laughing hysterically. "Honey, I'm home!" he screamed while kicking over furniture and slashing at pictures on the walls. "You'll never guess who I ran into out in the woods this morning!" He slashed the curtains on the windows and kicked over the kitchen table as he rounded the corner. "Your tree hugger and me had a little run-in, and he got the long end of the blade, you could say!"

Had the frying pan Abby slammed into Nash's forehead been any heavier, it might have killed him. But it was small and in his crazed state only sufficient to knock him down long enough for her to scoot past him and flee out the front door. She ran around to the rear of the house, hoping that she could enter the woods and hide.

But Nash recovered quickly. He opened the back door and caught her with a leap from the back porch rail. The fall knocked the breath out of Abby. She could feel his hands around her shoulders as she tumbled through wet leaves. She gasped for air and struggled to stand. But it was no use. She was exhausted.

"Get up!" Nash stood over her and shouted. "I said, get up and get back in the cabin!" He shoved her in the ribs with the toe of his shoe.

Abby slowly rose to her knees. "You'll have to kill me first," she said defiantly.

Nash's face filled with rage. His eyes bulged when he screamed his anger over the thunder and jerked Abby to her feet by her hair. He pulled her face close to his and spoke with cruel confidence. "First things first." His eyes peered down her shirt and then back to her face.

But Abby was not afraid of him. He could see that on her face. But not in her eyes—her eyes were looking past him.

Glowering, he turned and, in that instant, he froze in fear. "You're dead!" he shouted as he began backing away. "I killed you!"

Abby ran to Sherrod. The blood stains on his shirt alarmed her, but when she pulled his shirt back, there were no wounds. She clung to his arm. "Be careful. He has a knife." Her voice was trembling.

"I know," Sherrod responded. But he did not look at her. He was focused on Nash. "Stand behind me," he said as he walked toward the man who was backing into the woods.

"You're dead!" Nash shouted, his back against a tree. "You're not here." He wanted to believe his own words.

But when Sherrod raised his hand and lightning

crackled in the sky above them, Nash turned and ran into the woods. Thunder pounded the air until he covered his ears and screamed. The wind swirled through the woods, tossing down dead trees and branches in his path. He ran for his life, with no sense of direction until he came to a rock outcrop. He looked frantically for a way down. There was none. Confused, he ran back toward the edge of the woods, but a tree fell in his path, its thick, dead branches blocking him. Shaking with fear, he stopped in his tracks and realized he was not alone. He turned and saw Sherrod standing on the outcrop. The storm was still raging, but the sky was brightening over the mountains. Nash could see Buena Vista in the distance. His life had come to this. He dropped on his knees and pointed his knife at Sherrod. "You don't know what I've done!" he shouted. "You can't see what I am."

Sherrod did not blink an eye when he responded, "In the flicker of a bolt of lightning I saw what you are, dark heart. And I know what you have done. But this is where it ends."

Nash stood up slowly. He crouched. "I killed you already. I won."

Sherrod watched Nash's eyes. "You misjudged me." He waited for the attack he knew would come.

When Nash charged at him with raised knife, Sherrod put one foot behind him to brace his stance. But Nash was strong in his rage and the last sound Sherrod heard as the two stumbled off the rock ledge was a boom of thunder.

Abby cleared the woods just in time to see Doc

rush toward the outcrop. She gasped and froze in her tracks. "No!" she heard Doc shout.

"My God!" Charles Pauley ran up behind Doc, his smoking gun still in his hand.

Doc looked over the ledge and saw Nash's body thirty feet below, mangled and impaled on the sharp, dead branches of a tree. His forehead had been blown away by Charles' bullet. The snap of a branch drew his attention. "Hold on to my feet, Charley!" he called as he lay down on his stomach and pushed himself over the lip of the rock.

"Come help me, Abby." Charles gripped Doc's ankles and braced himself.

Abby ran to Charles.

"Hold the back of my coat, Abby," Charles instructed her as he inched closer to the ledge. "We've got you, Doc. Go ahead."

Abby held on tight. "Sherrod's alive, Charles. Doc will get him." She prayed under her breath as the men struggled.

Sherrod had somehow become entangled in a series of weaving tree roots and vines that protruded out of a crevice in the rock wall five feet below. The roots were breaking under the strain of his weight, and he was trying to force his fingers into a jagged and thin crevice when he heard Doc's voice from above and then saw Doc's hand reaching down to him.

"Take my hand, son," Doc spoke calmly and reassuringly. "I won't let you go."

Sherrod looked up and saw Doc's face. Below him were sharp rocks and the lifeless body of Nash

Moseley. He let go of the breaking roots and put his life in the firm grasp of his father's hand.

A minute later, Sherrod rolled over the lip of the rock and into Abby's arms.

Tired and breathless, Doc patted Charles on the back. "Ed Conner is going to have a lot of sorting out to do, Charley." He wrapped his coat around Abby's shoulders.

For a long while, they all sat there in the rain as the storm passed over Buena Vista.

Epilogue

Emily Tynes lived to see Sherrod and Abby's wedding in the meadow that fall of 1958. It was a sunny day when Charles Pauley drove her and Doc up to the meadow in Woodrow Marsden's old horse-drawn buggy. Never before had there been so many folks in the highland meadow. There was a lot of good food and singing. Abby played her guitar and sang songs she had learned from the radio, along with some that she had written.

Reverend Roy Thomas from the Buena Vista Baptist Church performed the ceremony. And the children's choir sang beautifully. The trees were in rare radiant fall color that year. Soon they would retreat into themselves, the brilliance of their nature subdued.

In the summer of 1959, a baby was born in the cabin on the mountain, and Emily held her namesake in her arms. That in itself was worth waiting for.

The mountains were green and lush when Emily Tynes died. But Jonathan, the walnut tree that grew outside her bedroom window and was used to hearing her voice, shed half its foliage in the days following her passing. Sherrod told Doc and Abby that Jonathan was grieving her loss.

One night that fall after putting little Emmy to bed in the warmth of the cabin on Elephant Mountain, Frank Tynes sat down in the den and began reading a newly-published book by Abby Rhode Dane. He smiled when he whispered its title, *Moonglow*.

Outside in the meadow Sherrod and Abby lay in each other's arms on a blanket, gazing up at the night sky. Early stars had bowed to the brilliance of a harvest moon.

"Have you heard what is said about the Shenandoah Valley, Abby?"

Abby turned her head and looked at the profile of her husband's face. "Tell me," she answered.

Sherrod smiled. "Well, it is said that the beauty of the valley so awed the heavens, that each star cast the brightest jewel from its own crown into the valley's limpid waters, there to sparkle and shine ever after in a gesture of celestial benediction."

Abby was amazed at the beauty of his description. "Did you write that?" She turned on her side and snuggled close to him.

He kissed her forehead. "No. It's an old Indian legend. But I have always loved it."

Abby thought about the legend. "The stars have given us so much beauty."

Sherrod smiled. "But the moon gave me you."

Later that night as the wind caressed the hillsides, Abby sang softly the song she had learned from her mother so long ago.

And the trees danced in moonglow.

Titles by Francis Eugene Wood

The Wooden Bell (A Christmas Story)
The Legend of Chadega and the Weeping Tree
Wind Dancer's Flute
The Crystal Rose
The Angel Carver
The Fodder Milo Stories
The Nipkins (Trilogy)
Snowflake (A Christmas Story)
The SnowPeople
Return to Winterville
Winterville Forever
Autumn's Reunion (A Story of Thanksgiving)
The Teardrop Fiddle
Two Tales and a Pipe Dream
The Christmas Letter
Tackle Box Memories
Moonglow

These books are available through the author's
Website: www.tipofthemoon.com
Email address: fewwords@moonstar.com

Write to:
Tip-of-the-Moon Publishing Company
175 Crescent Road
Farmville, Virginia 23901

Virginia author Francis Eugene Wood has published nineteen books since 1996 through his Tip-of-the-Moon Publishing Company, which he operates with his wife, Chris, from their home in Buckingham County, Virginia. The award-winning author has been called "prolific" and "a natural storyteller." He is known for his rich depictions of rural Virginia life and his unique ability to blend fact and fiction in a way that mirrors the world around him.